Seventeen Coffins

Philip Caveney

Published by Fledgling Press 2014

Cover Design: Kylie Tesdale
lalliusmaximus.wix.com/kylietesdale

Printed and bound by:
DS Smith Print Solutions, Glasgow

ISBN: 9781905916744

This book is for Clare Cain at Fledgling Press who saw the potential in *Crow Boy* and worked so hard to make it a reality. It's also for Kylie Tesdale, who did such a brilliant job with the cover art.

Foreword

In July, 1836, a group of boys, hunting for rabbits on the slopes of Arthur's Seat, the picturesque hill that overlooks the city of Edinburgh, made a strange accidental discovery. In a hidden recess in the rocks, they found seventeen tiny coffins. Sadly, the boys didn't fully appreciate what a remarkable find this was and spent some time amusing themselves by throwing the coffins at each other. In the process they managed to destroy more than half of them.

Luckily, they happened to mention their find to one of their teachers, a Mr Ferguson, who was a member of an archaeological society. He promptly climbed the hill and gathered up what was salvageable, just eight coffins. When he got home, he carefully prised up the coffin lids to find that each of them contained a tiny dressed doll. Afterwards, the coffins found their way into the hands of a private collector and many years later, to the National Museum of Scotland, where they can still be seen today.

Over the years many historians have wondered what the coffins might signify. Who made them and hid them in that secret recess? And more importantly, why?

Nobody has come up with a definitive answer — until now.

One

Tom went down the last few steps and followed the party of tourists through a gloomy entrance. He found himself standing, once again, on Mary King's Close. He looked expectantly around. It was just as he remembered it: the steeply sloping street, the lines of filthy washing hanging overhead, the rough plastered walls rearing up to the concrete roof high above him. He felt, more than anything else, a sharp jolt of disappointment. He wasn't sure what he'd expected to find down here. Something more than just a seventeenth century street.

'So this is the place you've been so mad to visit?' said Mum. 'I can see why. It's very atmospheric.'

He nodded, but didn't reply. When he'd agreed to spend part of his summer holidays in Edinburgh with Mum and Hamish, it had always been in his mind that he'd pay this place a second visit. He was looking for something here, but he wasn't sure yet exactly what it was.

'I must say I'm surprised you wanted to come back,' continued Mum. 'After the accident, I would have thought you'd want to stay well away. What is it about this place that attracts you?'

Tom frowned. He couldn't really explain everything to her. How would it sound?

'Well, Mum, see, the last time I was here, it was like,

1645? There was bubonic plague in the close and I was apprenticed to a guy who wore a mask and called himself Doctor Rae . . . only he wasn't the real Doctor Rae, he was this crook called William McSweeny . . .'

Yeah, that'd go down well. He pictured Mum edging nervously away from him, looking for the nearest exit. And it wasn't even as if he could show her the photograph that used to be on his mobile, the photograph of a girl called Morag. In the picture, she'd been sitting at the table in Missie Grierson's filthy kitchen, smiling up at him and asking him what he was doing, because there were no such things as phones in 1645 and the idea of a photograph was something she could never have understood. A miniature, she'd called it, and remarked how you couldn't even see the brush strokes. Thinking about it now seemed somehow ridiculous and yet, the photograph had been there on his mobile when he woke up in the hospital. It was the last thing he remembered looking at before he dropped back into a dreamless sleep. But when he'd awoken and looked again, the picture had already started to fade, and it had continued to do so, a little more each time he'd looked, until finally, after a few days, all that remained of Morag was a pale grey rectangle.

The photograph had faded but the memory of her was still fresh in his mind and he'd thought that maybe if he came back here, he might somehow be able to get near to her again, might be able to say sorry for not looking after her well enough.

'You're probably wondering what this place is,' said a voice and looking up, Tom saw that Agnes Chambers had taken up her position, smiling at the group of thirty or so tourists in front of her. 'What we're looking at here are the streets of the old city under the Royal Mile, just as they would have looked in the 1600s.' It was a different Agnes Chambers than Tom remembered, though the maid's costume was exactly the same and so was the script.

'I wonder if they've got any jobs going here?' muttered Mum. 'I could easily do what she's doing.'

Tom refrained from pointing out that the girl playing Agnes was in her early twenties and probably had some acting experience to go with it. He knew only too well that Mum was on the lookout for work. Judging by the strained atmosphere at Hamish's house over the past few days, Tom reckoned that things weren't working out too well for Mum and Hamish.

'Now we'll go and visit the houses of some of the people who lived here in the 1600s,' announced Agnes.

She led the group down the hill and through the doorway of a chamber where a realistic-looking waxwork effigy of a masked man, Dr Rae, was bent over the figure of a child in a bed, inspecting the symptoms of bubonic plague. Several of the tourists gave gasps of revulsion, but Tom could have assured them that this was nothing like as bad as the real thing.

'He looks a real charmer,' muttered Mum.

'Yeah, he was,' agreed Tom and then realised that

Mum was giving him an odd look. 'I . . . read about him at school,' he added. 'We did a project.'

'A project about Edinburgh? In Manchester?'

'Er . . . sure, why not? Edinburgh's cool.'

There were some shushing sounds from the other tourists, so they fell silent while Agnes talked them through the symptoms of bubonic plague and explained how the Doctor would slice open the red swellings with a razor, squeeze out the pus and then cauterise the wounds with a red hot poker. Mum's face was a picture as she said this. Tom found himself thinking that what Agnes couldn't describe, or even know about, was the awful smell of burning flesh that filled the room at such a time.

He was glad when this part of the tour was over and Agnes led them on, along narrow corridors to the doorway of the room he'd most wanted to visit on this trip.

'We call this little Annie's room,' said Agnes, and Tom wanted to interrupt and tell her: No, you got that bit wrong. This is Morag's room. It's her ghost that haunts this spot because it's near where she died, murdered by William McSweeny, the man who died after falling through a roof. A man that I killed with my own hands. But Tom knew if he said anything about any of it, the whole party would look at him as if he were mad, so he held his tongue and followed the queue of people into the little room.

He steeled himself, expecting . . . what? That a cold hand would reach out and touch him? That he'd see Morag's flickering image standing in a corner, gazing up at him with the same affection she'd shown him in life?

That he would hear her voice speaking to him across the distance of time?

But no, once again he was disappointed. There was just the little room, the open wooden chest and a great mound of bedraggled dolls and cuddly toys, left there by an endless procession of tourists. Mum gazed down at the offerings with a look of faint disgust on her face.

'That lot looks like it could do with a good wash,' she said and any spell that might have existed down there, was completely broken.

'Come on,' said Tom, turning away. 'I've seen enough.' He led Mum towards the door, pushing past the other tourists. Mum followed, mystified.

'I don't understand,' she said. 'You nagged me for days to bring you here and it's really interesting . . .'

'It's not what I expected,' he said, not looking back at her. 'It's . . . different than I remember. Let's find the way out.'

'Shouldn't we wait for the rest of the group?' asked Mum. 'We could get lost down here.'

'I know the way,' he assured her. 'It's just–'

He broke off as he saw something moving at the far end of a long corridor; a tall dark figure clad in a leather cloak. In one gloved hand it carried a lantern which burned with an eerie glow and in the other hand, a long white stick. The hooded head turned to look at them and Tom saw the familiar masked face, the long, crow-like bill. The figure began to move, striding towards them, seeming to float above the hard earth floor. Tom's heart pounded in his chest like a drum and a terrible coldness settled over him. He grabbed Mum's arm, squeezing it so hard that she gave a gasp of pain.

11

'Tom! What are you–'

He opened his mouth to tell her to run, but nothing came out and when he tried to stir his legs into motion, he found that they could barely hold him upright. The vision swept closer, the goggle-rimmed eyes glaring at Tom as though they had recognised an old friend, looking at him the same way they had examined him when they searched for the right spot to bury the blade of a knife . . . Then the figure was lifting the lantern to illuminate Tom's face and a muffled voice, with a soft Edinburgh accent, spoke from behind the mask.

'Can I help you at all?'

'I . . . I . . .' Tom struggled to get words out.

'You seem to have wandered away from the rest of the group,' said the man and Tom realised with a rush of relief that it was just one of the staff, dressed up in seventeenth-century costume.

'We were looking for the way out,' said Mum helpfully. 'Bit claustrophobic down here.'

There was a deep chuckle from behind the mask which, despite everything, served to send a chill down Tom's spine.

'It's not everyone's cup of tea.' The man lifted the lantern. 'Just follow the corridor there and you'll see an exit on your left.' The masked head bowed and the figure moved on its way.

Mum smiled. 'Wouldn't fancy his job. Must be hot as anything under that all that gear.' She looked down at Tom. 'Are you all right? You're *shaking*.'

'I'm fine,' he insisted, without much conviction.

'Come on.' He led her along the corridor as they'd been directed and pushed through the exit door. Stone steps led them upwards and they emerged into the reassuring light and warmth of the gift shop. A man in a frock coat and knee breeches greeted them at the door. 'Everything OK?' he asked them. He gave Mum a sympathetic look. 'Some people can find the place a bit unnerving.'

'We just needed some air,' Tom assured him as he hurried past.

'Did you want a souvenir?' Mum asked him, but he kept walking towards the exit.

'I've already got one,' he assured her.

She caught up with him in the narrow alleyway outside.

'What is wrong with you?' she asked him. 'We were only in there five minutes. I was expecting to make a day of it.'

Tom shrugged. 'Sorry,' he said. 'I just . . . it wasn't what I was looking for.'

'But you've been here before,' she reminded him. 'Surely you must have known what it would be like. So, why . . .?'

Tom stared at his shoes. 'It's complicated,' he said. How could he explain to her what he really felt? That going back to Mary King's Close had felt somehow like something from his past. Like Timeslyp, the computer game he'd played so avidly only a year ago. Then, it had seemed so exciting. Now, whenever he revisited the game on his mobile phone, it felt somehow irrelevant – because a real trip back in time was so much more immersive; something that affected every sense – sight, sound, even smell. And returning to Mary King's Close had felt similarly disappointing. The doorway into the past had been well and truly shut. 'I was just . . . expecting something more,' he said, at last. Like the first time I went there, he thought.

'Well . . .' Mum reached into the pocket of her coat and pulled out a guidebook. 'There's lots of other stuff to do in Edinburgh. And I'm not really ready to head back to Fairmilehead just yet.' She studied the book for a moment, then looked at Tom and smiled. 'Tell you what,' she said. 'How do you feel about the National Museum of Scotland?'

Two

Tom had to admit there was a lot to see here. He and Mum wandered silently through the huge Victorian galleries, each of them packed with what could only be described as wonders. Complete dinosaur skeletons loomed over them like beasts risen from a nightmare. A life-size shark seemed to float in the air above their heads, like some uncanny zeppelin, armed not with machine guns, but with row upon row of glittering, razor-sharp teeth. Here were books bound in human skin, the titles tattooed in blue-black ink. There were suits of armour, glinting dully in their glass cases and beside them, the weapons of medieval warfare – swords, shields, crossbows. And more. So much more!

Caskets and jewels, uniforms and weapons, posters and paintings. Wizened Egyptian mummies wrapped in mouldering bandages gazed blindly up from their decorated caskets. Waxwork kings and queens sat upon glittering thrones, surveying their subjects in silent disdain.

And there were animals! Bears and wolves, giraffes and lions – as real as life, but completely motionless. There was even a huge African elephant, gazing down at Tom with dark, friendly eyes as though inviting him to clamber up onto his back and take a stroll through the nearest jungle.

Eventually, it was all too much to take in and they found themselves exploring some of the quieter rooms upstairs, threading their way past glass cases that bristled with ancient relics and treasures. It was in one such room, up on the fourth floor, that they discovered the coffins.

'Look at those!' said Mum, pointing to the glass case in which they rested. There they were, arranged in a row and lit up by tiny spotlights; eight miniature wooden coffins, perhaps a hundred millimetres in length and each of them containing a little wooden doll, dressed in crudely fashioned clothes. The coffin lids were arranged alongside them, decorated with oddly-shaped metal emblems.

'Weird,' said Tom. He read the little card positioned beside them. 'Says here there used be seventeen of them,' he told Mum, who had walked around to the far side of the glass cabinet. 'Some kids found them in 1836 on Arthur's Seat.' He looked at his Mum enquiringly. 'That's the mountain, isn't it?'

She nodded. 'We could take a walk up there later if you wanted,' she told him. 'It's a nice day and I'm told it's not so hard if you take your time.'

Tom returned his attention to the card. 'Says here the kids didn't know they were worth anything and started throwing them at each other!' He laughed, picturing the scene. 'That's why there's only eight coffins left. But this schoolteacher realised they were important, so . . .' Tom glanced up again. Mum was looking at him through the glass, gazing at him with a fierce intensity.

'What?' he grunted.

'How's your dad getting on?' she asked him. He was surprised. It was the first time she'd mentioned Dad this holiday.

'He's . . . ok, I guess.'

She nodded, but kept staring. 'Is he, you know . . . seeing anyone?'

Tom felt uncomfortable. This was grown up stuff, which he tried to avoid whenever possible. But he didn't think he should lie to her.

'Er . . . yeah, he is actually. Her name's Ruth. An English teacher. She's nice.'

Mum nodded again. 'That's . . . great,' she said, but she didn't look or sound as if she was pleased. 'Really great. I'm . . . glad for him. Have you met her?'

He shrugged. 'We've been out for dinner and stuff. She's ok.'

He made a valiant attempt to change the subject. He pointed to the card. 'It says here, the remaining coffins fell into the hands of a private collector, but they were donated to the museum in 1901.'

Mum made no move to indicate that she had heard what he said. She was staring down at the coffins now, lost in thought. Tom felt moved to break the silence.

'Mum, is everything all right? With you and Hamish, I mean?'

Her eyes refocused. 'Oh, sure,' she said, making a dismissive gesture. 'We're good. I suppose it's just . . . well, I thought I'd find work easily up here and . . . it's taking a lot longer than I expected. Hamish travels so much with his job, and I'm on my own quite a bit so I . . .' She waved a hand again, as though she'd just remembered something. 'He might be joining us in a bit, actually. Hamish. He was tired this morning so I left him asleep, but I texted him on the way here, told him where we'd be. If he fancies coming.' She smiled. 'That's ok, isn't it?'

'Sure, whatever.' But Tom felt a twinge of irritation. He'd never warmed to Hamish and that was before he'd encountered a seventeenth-century villain called William McSweeny who shared Hamish's face and voice. Tom doubted that the present-day Hamish was anything like as villainous as his counterpart, but there was still something about the man he'd never liked and probably never would. He continued reading the card.

'Nobody's sure who put the coffins up there. There are theories though. Some people thought it might be witches. You know, like voodoo dolls or something. Or it could be they're for sailors that drowned at sea. It says here–'

'There you are! I've been looking everywhere for you!'

Tom lifted his head as the sound of a strident voice rudely interrupted the peace and quiet. He saw Hamish striding between the cabinets, towards them. His shoulders were hunched inside his khaki jacket and he had a cross expression on his slab of a face. 'God's sake, woman. I must have rung your phone a dozen times. Kept going straight to voicemail.'

Mum looked back at him. 'Sorry, I had it on silent. They don't like you to use mobiles in here. I didn't think.'

'That's your problem, you never think.' He stepped past Tom and went around to the other side of the display cabinet to stand face-to-face with Mum. 'I thought maybe you were avoiding me,' he growled. He glanced through the glass at Tom without making any comment then returned his attention to her. 'Have you any idea how many rooms there are in this blasted place? I must have looked in all of them.'

'I'm sorry. We were just looking at these coffins, here. Amazing, don't you think?'

Hamish grunted. 'Never mind about that. I've got Hibs tickets for this afternoon. Jimmy sorted them out for me.'

Mum seemed almost relieved. 'Oh well, that's . . . great. You go ahead then. Me and Tom can entertain ourselves, can't we?'

Hamish looked irritated. 'No, you numpty! I've got tickets for all of us. Had to move heaven and earth to get them. I said we'd meet Jimmy and the lads in The Feathers before the match, for a few wee gargles. If we go now, we should be in time.'

'Oh.' Mum looked uncertainly at Tom. 'But I . . . I don't think Tom's very keen on football.'

Hamish snorted. 'Is that a fact?' He glanced at Tom again, as though inspecting some lower form of insect life. 'Now, why doesn't that surprise me? It'll do him good to get out in the fresh air. If you ask me he spends too much time indoors, playing computer games and watching the telly. That's why he's got no colour. And excuse me, but I seem to recall that the last time he visited one of these historical places, he ended up in hospital.'

'Yes, but . . . you surely can't mind me wanting to spend a bit of quality time with my son? We were really enjoying the –'

'Wheesht, woman! You can spend quality time with him at the football match. Now come on, we're wasting good drinking time here.' He reached out a hand and grabbed Mum by the arm.

'Hamish, no! I'd really rather stay here, if you don't mind.'

'Don't be ridiculous. Have you any idea how much those tickets cost me? Come on.' He started to pull her towards the exit. Tom felt moved enough to walk around the glass cabinet to her aid.

'She doesn't want to go,' he said.

Hamish gave him a scornful look. 'What's it got to do with you?' he asked. He looked at Mum. 'Ok, so let the kid stay here and we'll go to the match. He's old enough to look after himself.'

'That's not the point. I haven't seen him in months. Now, please. You go and let us stay here. I'm sure you'll find a buyer for the tickets.'

Hamish's voice dropped to a threatening snarl. 'I'm not telling you again,' he said. 'We're going to the match, with or without him. Get used to the idea.'

Tom stepped forward and put a hand on Hamish's arm. Up close, he could smell the whisky fumes on the man's breath.

'Let go of her,' he said, with a firmness that surprised him.

'Get lost,' Hamish told him. He slapped Tom's hand away, but Tom put it right back.

'I said, "Leave her alone."' he repeated.

'Tom, don't,' said Mum, urgently, as though she knew what would happen next.

But it was already too late.

Hamish didn't hit Tom. He just put a hand to his chest and pushed, hard. Tom felt himself falling backwards, his feet gone from under him. He saw Mum's horrified expression, saw her open her mouth to shout something, but then a point of fire seemed to explode at the back of his head; a point of fire that spread suddenly and explosively to engulf him. For an instant, the world shimmered and shuddered around him like a mirage. And then he was falling, he was falling headlong into blackness and there was something horribly familiar about the sensation, because he'd felt this once before and he would have spent time thinking about the implications, except that a total blackness slipped over his head like a hood and he knew no more.

Three

I'm back. The thought shuddered through his conscious mind as he gradually returned to his senses; the treacly darkness giving way to a shifting, shimmering red. He opened his eyes and wasn't entirely surprised to find himself staring up at a narrow strip of blue sky. He tried to move his head and a stinging sensation at the top of his skull made him wince. He lifted the fingers of one hand to probe at the injury and the tips came away stained red.

He took stock of his situation. He appeared to be lying in a narrow alleyway, stretched on his back amidst a heap of foul-smelling rubbish, but he knew instantly that this was not the kind of rubbish you'd expect to find in the modern world. There were no bin bags here, no printed cardboard containers, just a heap of old bones, fish heads and vegetable peelings; the combined stink of which quickly filled his nostrils and persuaded him to make a move. He tried to get up and had to wait for a moment for a spell of dizziness to recede. As his head cleared he sat up and looked quickly around. Dirty brick walls stood close on either side of him, and a narrow alleyway led to a flight of stone steps at the far end. They went up a long way and from where he was sitting he couldn't see what was at the top of them.

He knew he was no longer in his own time and he was surprised to find that he was oddly excited at the prospect. Maybe he'd meet up with some old friends again. Cameron. Missie Grierson. *Maybe even Morag* . . . but then he reminded himself that Morag was dead and any sense of hope he'd had instantly evaporated. He got to his feet and stood for a moment, brushing scraps of rubbish from the back of his jeans and wondering what to do next. The alleyway seemed to beckon to him, so he walked along it and when he got to the end, he crossed a narrow street that stretched across his path from left to right and began to climb the long flight of steps.

He emerged onto another street, where rough-timbered houses crowded in close upon each other and now he was convinced he had gone back in time. There were no road signs in evidence; no parking spaces, no telegraph poles, just two rows of tumbledown dwellings and chimneys that belched grey smoke. He heard the sound of children, laughing and shouting, and turned his head to look in that direction. He saw a young man standing in the cobbled street off to his left; a thin, ragged fellow with a mop of curly brown hair. He was probably eighteen or nineteen years old, Tom decided, dressed in what must once have been a respectable black suit; a tailcoat and a pair of trousers, but the trousers were ragged around the ankles and the youth had no shoes or socks on his feet. Around his neck he wore a bright red spotted scarf, the only splash of colour in his entire outfit. He was surrounded by four or five children, every one of them as ragged as he, but much younger. They were pulling at the tails of his coat and teasing him, chanting the words, 'Daft Jamie, Daft Jamie!' over and over. He kept trying to catch them, but he moved awkwardly, limping on one leg and they were able to dance easily away from his clutches, mocking him as they did so.

Tom looked hopefully around, but there was no sign of anyone else who might be able to help the youth so he felt obliged to do something himself. He started towards the little scene, rubbing his aching head as he did so. As he drew closer, he raised his voice to shout.

'Oi! You lot. Leave him alone!'

The children, clearly startled, took to their heels without even looking at him, leaving the youth scowling after them and waving a fist in their general direction.

'Are you all right?' Tom asked as he drew close.

The youth turned and looked at him in slack-jawed amazement, as though witnessing some kind of miracle. Tom quickly understood his surprise. His 21st century outfit of t-shirt, quilted jacket, jeans and trainers must have looked pretty odd in this setting.

'Did they hurt you?' Tom asked.

The youth shook his head and spoke, in a strange stammering voice. 'They c . . . can't hurt Jamie,' he said. 'They c . . . can try, but Jamie is too c . . . clever for them.' He took a hesitant step closer to Tom and reached out a finger to trace one of the letters on his t-shirt, which spelled out the word iManc. It was just a design that was doing the rounds in Manchester, but to Jamie it seemed to have some deeper significance.

'You are a walking b . . . b . . . book,' he said. 'If I could read, I would r . . . r . . . read you.'

Tom tried to smile, but his head was throbbing and what emerged was probably more of a grimace.

Jamie tilted his head to one side. 'Wh . . . what's your name?' he asked.

'Tom. Tom Afflick.'

'T . . . Tom Afflick,' said Jamie, saying the words slowly, as though he was unsure of them. 'The w . . . walking book.'

Tom shrugged his shoulders. 'Whatever,' he said. 'Where exactly are we?'

Jamie looked around, open-mouthed for a moment, as though not quite sure himself. Then he pointed a finger at the cobbles beneath him. 'We are *here*,' he said solemnly.

'Er . . . yeah, sure. But what I mean is . . .' Tom made an attempt to think logically. 'This is Edinburgh, right?'

Jamie nodded. 'Of course,' he said. ''Last t . . . time I checked.'

'And . . . what year is it, exactly?'

Jamie stared at him. 'It is . . . *this* year,' he said, with great certainty and smiled proudly. Tom tried not to groan. Of all the people he could have met, why did it have to be this guy?

'No,' he said. 'No, you don't understand. I mean the date. It's . . . sixteen forty five, yes?'

'Is it?' Jamie looked puzzled. 'That's strange. I thought it was eighteen t . . . t . . . twenty eight.'

Now it was Tom's turn to be bewildered. 'It can't be,' he said.

But Jamie was reaching into the pocket of his tattered jacket. He pulled out a small brass box and showed it to Tom. 'My c . . . c . . . calendar,' he said.

Tom looked at it doubtfully. 'That's not a calendar, that's a box.'

Jamie shook his head. 'Oh aye,' he said. 'Snuffbox.' He flipped up the lid and showed Tom the contents. 'You'll take a pinch?' When Tom shook his head, he took out a little copper spoon which he used to lift a large measure up to his nose. He sniffed it up, paused for a moment and then sneezed loudly. He used one of the ends of the kerchief around his neck to wipe his nose, something that made Tom feel slightly ill. He closed the lid of the box and returned it to his pocket, but kept the spoon in his hand. 'A snuffbox, but also a c . . . c . . . calendar,' he announced. He held the spoon out so that Tom could see that there were seven small holes punched into the handle of it. 'See?' Now Jamie placed the fingers of his other hand on the holes and began to move them in a strange and complicated rhythm, as though counting. He did this for quite some time, his brow furrowed in concentration, before announcing,

'T . . . today, is . . .' His fingers moved a few times more, 'September the ninth, eighteen t . . . t . . . twenty eight.' Then he grinned, displaying rows of rotten, misshapen teeth. He seemed very pleased with himself.

'Right,' said Tom. 'Of course it is.' He took a deep

breath. Ok, he told himself, the thing was not to panic. He'd gone back in time and that had happened to him before, so he just had to wait it out until something happened to send him back again, which hopefully wouldn't be too long. Meanwhile, he just needed to keep his head down and stay out of trouble. One thing was for sure. This weirdo who used a snuffbox as a dodgy calendar, clearly couldn't be trusted. Tom needed to find somebody else, somebody who actually knew what they were talking about. 'I've got to get moving,' he announced and turning, he began to walk away.

'W . . . wait!' said Jamie. He pulled the box from his pocket, returned the spoon to it and put it away. 'Where are you going?'

Tom could only shrug his shoulders. 'I don't know. I'm . . . lost,' he said. 'I need to try and find out exactly where I am.'

'You're in the W . . . W . . . West Port,' said Jamie.

This meant nothing to Tom. He kept walking along the street and Jamie fell into a limping step beside him, keeping up with great difficulty.

'There's no need to come with me,' Tom assured him. 'Really. You can just get on with whatever it is you were doing.'

Jamie shook his head. 'You h . . . helped me, so I'll help you.' He pointed at Tom. 'You're not from E . . . Edinburgh,' he observed.

'Well spotted, Sherlock,' said Tom. They emerged onto a wider, busier street and there, towering above them, was the great hulking grey shape of the castle, so it was clear that he was now some distance from his original starting point in the museum. This reminded him of what had happened just before he'd left. Hamish and Mum. He needed to get back there and help her out as soon as possible. Only that was easier said than done.

'Are you a S . . . S . . . S . . .?'

'Yeah, yeah, I'm a Sassenach,' said Tom irritably. It was a name he'd been called several times on his last trip and he knew it wasn't intended as a compliment.

Jamie shook his head. 'I was g . . . going to say, are you a sailor?' He waved a hand at Tom's clothes. 'You look like you c . . . came off a boat.'

'We all dress like this in Manchester,' said Tom. He studied the street for a while, looking at the people walking up and down it. He was beginning to think that Jamie was right about the date. They looked quite different to the ragged creatures he'd encountered in the seventeenth century. The men were wearing tailcoats, waistcoats and top hats. The women had bonnets and fancy dresses, and many of them wore white lace gloves. They were parading grandly up and down the street, making the most of the sunshine. A horse and carriage came clattering along the street, but the vehicle looked more elegant than the rough horse-drawn vehicles he had seen on his last trip and the coachman wore a fancy-looking uniform.

'M . . . M . . . Manchester, England?' asked Jamie, demanding Tom's attention once again and he nodded.

'Huh? Oh, yeah. Manchester, England.'

'I used to know a man from M . . . Manchester,' said Jamie brightly. He added, 'He died. He got d . . . drunk one night and fell into the loch.'

'That's nice,' said Tom, bleakly. Further up the street he spotted a ragged boy selling newspapers from a stand, shouting his wares as he did so.

'Edinburgh Chronicle. Get your latest edition!'

Tom hurried towards the boy and Jamie limped dutifully after him. Tom reached the stand and grabbed one of the papers from the pile. It didn't look like any newspaper he'd ever seen before, the pages huge, the printing tiny and crammed into scores of little columns. The boy looked at him, outraged.

'You going to pay for that?' he demanded.

'I only need it for a minute,' Tom assured him. 'Relax.' He scanned the front page until he found a date up at the top. September the ninth, 1828. Tom handed the paper back to the boy and looked at Jamie with new respect. 'You were right,' he said. 'About the date.'

Jamie was indignant. 'Of course I was r . . . right,' he said.

'But . . . that means I've lost nearly . . . two hundred years.'

Jamie looked at him in dismay. 'Must have left it s . . . somewhere,' he said, and he made a big show of searching his pockets.

Tom smiled despite himself. 'No, I'm just saying the last time I came back it was a different date. It was 1645 . . .' He thought for a moment. He remembered the little coffins he'd been looking at in the museum, just before he'd fallen. Did they have something to do with this? He tried to remember what had been on the printed card in the glass case. He thought it had said they'd been found in 1836, but that would be around eight years from now. Still, he told himself, who was to say that the coffins hadn't been hidden up on Arthur's Seat for all that time? Maybe he'd come to 1828 because it was the year when the coffins were made. Why else this particular time and place? Oh, sure, he could tell himself that he was just unconscious and dreaming all this. That's what everyone had told him last time it had happened. Which would have been fine, if it hadn't been for that photograph of Morag . . .

This thought prompted him into action. He reached into his coat pocket and pulled out his mobile, noting as he did so that the battery level was at the midway mark. He tapped the camera icon, lifted the phone and snapped a quick picture of Jamie, who was staring into the lens in complete bafflement. Then he turned and took a couple more photographs; one of the street and another of the castle looming over them. This time, he told himself, when he got back – *if* he got back – the first thing he'd do would be to make copies of the photographs and print them out. Then he'd have proof of where he'd been.

'Wh . . . what are you doing?' asked Jamie.

Good question. Tom thought about trying to explain about mobile phones and digital images, but thought better of it. He was cold and hungry and he needed to start thinking about somewhere to sleep. There was no telling how long he'd be here and he didn't much fancy the idea of stretching himself out on the streets.

'Jamie, you said you'd help me, right?'

Jamie nodded.

'I need somewhere to stay,' said Tom. 'A room or something? A hotel. Can you help me find a place?'

Jamie looked doubtful. 'A room?' he muttered. He thought for a moment. 'There's my m . . . m . . . mother's house,' he said.

'You think I could stay there?' asked Tom hopefully.

Jamie shook his head. 'She doesn't even let m . . . m . . . me stay there,' he admitted. 'I *wouldn't* stay there.' He rubbed his bottom with one hand. 'She's t . . . too fond of the strap. She beat me once for eating bread.'

'She beat you for eating a slice of bread?' cried Tom, horrified.

'Ah, no. It was the whole loaf,' admitted Jamie. 'And then I accidentally knocked over a cupboard full of ch . . . ch . . . china.'

'So where *do* you stay?' Tom asked him.

Jamie waved a hand around. 'I know some g . . . good places,' he said. 'Out of the wind. S . . . s . . . safe places.'

Tom frowned. 'That's not the way I roll,' he said.

'Huh?'

'I mean . . . I like a roof over my head, you know? Walls around me.' He reached a hand into his pocket where his holiday money was stored, all twenty pounds of it. 'I can pay,' he added. He'd get around the problem of currency later. He'd managed to bribe a coachman in the seventeenth century with a five-pound note, simply by telling him it was English money. Which hadn't exactly been a lie.

Jamie pondered the matter for a moment and then he smiled.

'I'll take you to someone who m . . . might be able to help you,' he said. 'She's my f . . . f . . . friend.'

Tom raised his eyebrows. 'Your *girl* friend?' he ventured.

Jamie's face reddened. 'Wheesht!' he said. 'Not at all. Just a g . . . good friend. Come on, follow me.'

He turned and began to hobble back in the direction from which they'd come. Tom gazed after him for a moment and then shrugged his shoulders, deciding that at this stage in the game he had nothing much to lose. So he followed Jamie back along the street and down the long flight of steps. When they reached the bottom, instead of crossing the narrow road and going back into the dead end full of rubbish, Jamie turned right and led Tom through a brick archway where a grubby metal sign announced that they were now entering Tanner's Close.

Four

Tom followed Jamie into the close. It was narrow and gloomy, but it wasn't anything like as crowded as Mary King's Close had been and there wasn't the same network of wooden staircases on the outside of the tenements, linking the different floors to each other. Tom got the impression that, in the hundred and eighty five years that had passed since his last visit, attempts had been made to clean things up a bit. There were no pigs being butchered in the street, no barbers shaving their customers, and best of all, there was no longer an open sewer running down the middle of the street. All things to be grateful for. At the same time, he had to admit that the residents of this area seemed to be living far closer to each other than might be considered healthy.

As he walked along, he was aware of eyes examining him as he passed by, drawn no doubt to his casual clothes. Last time he'd ventured into the past he'd been dressed in his school uniform, which for some reason didn't seem to have attracted anything like as much attention. But now, as he wandered along the street, people were staring at him as though he was some kind of travelling exhibition and he felt like telling them to mind their own business. It soon became clear that nearly everybody on the close knew Jamie. He was greeted by everyone they passed, either with good-natured hellos or, as in the case of a gang of rough-looking teenage boys they chanced upon, a series of cruel insults, the gist of which seemed to be that Jamie was 'gone in the heed' and needed locking up. Tom glared at the boys and they moved on without causing any more trouble.

'Why do you let them talk to you like that?' Tom asked Jamie, and he just grinned.

'P . . . p . . . people who don't know me, say b . . . bad things,' he observed. 'It's b . . . because they're afraid that what I have might be c . . . c . . . catching.'

'They're just bullies,' said Tom, remembering something that Shona Grierson had once said to him. 'Stand up to them and they melt away like snowflakes in a microwave.'

'Oh aye,' said Jamie. 'True enough.' He thought for a moment. 'What's a m . . . m . . . m . . .?'

'Never mind,' said Tom. 'Where are we going, exactly?'

'We aren't going anywhere,' said Jamie.

Tom stared at him. 'How come?'

'Because we're already here.' Jamie indicated a doorway to his left. 'This is where my friends the M . . . McCallums live.' He looked at Tom. 'Do you know the McCallums?' he asked. 'Nicest family on T . . . Tanner's Close.'

'I don't know anyone in Edinburgh,' said Tom with absolute certainty. 'I used to know a few people but . . .

that was years ago. I don't think they'll be around any more.'

Jamie nodded as though he understood. He reached out a hand to a heavy doorknocker and rapped it several times. They waited for a few moments until the door opened and a woman looked out, a plump but pretty woman with shoulder length auburn hair and a smattering of freckles across the bridge of her nose. She smiled when she saw Jamie standing there.

'Well, well, wasn't I just thinking that it's been a while since we had a visit from Master Jamie?' she said. 'How have you been keeping?' She looked down disapprovingly. 'Still no shoes on those feet, I notice.'

'Oh, you know I d . . . don't like to wear shoes,' said Jamie.

'But this late summer isn't going to last forever,' she warned him. 'And then what will you do?' The woman's gaze flicked onto Tom and her blue eyes studied him with interest. The warm smile never faltered. 'And who is this with you?' she murmured. 'A new face, I think.'

'This is my friend, T . . . Tom,' announced Jamie, proudly. 'Some children were b . . . bothering me and Tom chased them off.'

'Did he now?' The woman seemed delighted at this news. 'Well, any friend of Master Jamie's is a friend of the McCallums. He's no kin to us, you understand, but we like to look out for him.' She extended a plump hand and shook Tom's hand 'I'm Mary McCallum and I'm very pleased to make your acquaintance.'

'Er . . . yeah, cool,' said Tom. 'Hiya.'

'Well, don't be standing there on the step, come along inside the pair of ye. You'll be staying for something to eat, I've no doubt?'

'Yes, please,' said Tom eagerly, realising how hungry he was. He and Jamie stepped into a narrow hallway.

'Good. It'll no' be much, but what we have, we're happy to share. Jamie, the children are up in the attic. Perhaps you'd like to take your friend up there and introduce him?'

'Of c . . . course, Mary. This way, Tom.' Jamie led Tom towards a narrow flight of stairs, while Mary strolled through a doorway into what looked like a dimly-lit kitchen.

'The McCallum's have b . . . been awfully kind to me,' said Jamie as they went up the steps. 'Ever since me and my Ma went our s . . . separate ways, they've always looked out for me. They are my d . . . dearest friends in the whole world.'

They reached a rickety landing and walked along it. At the very end there was a short flight of wooden steps. Jamie climbed them and Tom followed. They went through an arched doorway into a small attic room, where a girl and a boy, were sitting side by side at a rough wooden table. The boy appeared to be carving a piece of wood with a small sharp knife and there was what looked like a large collection of tiny toy soldiers ranged on the table in front of him. The girl was writing something into a notebook using a simple quill pen and inkwell. She was around Tom's age, he thought, tall and pretty with straight blonde hair and green eyes. He instantly knew that she must be Mary's daughter, the likeness was so marked. She looked up as the newcomers entered and smiled enchantingly.

'Look who's come to visit us, Fraser!' she exclaimed.

The boy must have been several years older than her. He too resembled Mary, though the unruly mop of hair that hung to his shoulders was black and his eyes dark brown. He reluctantly tore his gaze from the piece of wood he was carving. His eyes registered Jamie and then flicked challengingly across to Tom.

'Who the devil are you?' he asked, bluntly and the girl threw him an outraged look.

'Fraser, mind your manners!' she cried. 'In polite society you're supposed to wait for the visitors to speak first.'

'Oh, do *excuse* me!' sneered Fraser.

Jamie took the hint. 'T . . . Tom, may I introduce my friends Miss C . . . C . . . Catriona McCallum and her brother, Fraser.' He went over to crouch beside Fraser and started examining some of the wooden soldiers.

'Er . . . hi,' said Tom, unsure of the right words to use in such a situation. 'Tom Afflick. From . . . Manchester, UK. Er . . . Manchester, *England*.'

'An Englishman!' exclaimed Catriona excitedly. 'How interesting. Perhaps you'll be able to fill us in on all the latest English society gossip.'

Tom smiled helplessly. 'I wouldn't hold your breath,' he advised her; and Catriona and Fraser exchanged puzzled glances.

'Why would we do a thing like that?' asked Fraser.

'Er . . . never mind. It's just an expression. A . . . Manchester expression.'

'Excellent. *I wooden 'old yer breaf,*' repeated Catriona, trying to mimic Tom's Mancunian tones. 'That's a new one.' She turned to another page in her notebook and dipped her pen into the inkwell. 'You don't mind if I make a note of that, do you?'

'No,' said Tom. 'Er . . . why?'

Fraser rolled his eyes. 'Catriona makes a note of everything she hears,' he said, dismissively. 'She has books full of useless information. Shelves of them.'

'It's not useless,' Catriona informed him. 'It's fascinating.' She smiled at Tom. 'I collect unusual expressions.'

'Oh, yeah? That's cool,' said Tom.

'That's . . . cool,' murmured Catriona. And she wrote that down as well. Tom moved closer to the table to look over her shoulder. He saw that she had very neat handwriting, a far cry from the people he'd met last time around, none of whom could write anything more than their name.

'You obviously go to school,' he observed.

'We *used* to go to the Sessional School on Market Street,' said Catriona. 'But it was terrible. There were six hundred children there, you couldna learn anything.

So Da found us private tutors from the University. It costs a lot but he thinks it's worth it.'

'I suppose they call you Cat for short,' said Tom.

Catriona looked up at him, puzzled. 'No, they don't,' she said. 'Why, should they?'

'Umm . . . well, that's defo what we'd call you in Manchester anyway.'

'Cat,' she murmured. 'Yes, I rather like that. I think it's very unusual.' She looked at Fraser and Jamie. 'From now on, that's my name.'

'Sounds ridiculous,' said Fraser. 'Why not go the whole way and call yourself 'Dog'?'

'Or C . . . C . . . Cow!' giggled Jamie.

'Don't be so silly,' said Catriona. 'It's an English thing.' She smiled up at Tom. 'I wouldn't expect those two to understand. Do you think it suits me, Tom?'

'Er, yeah, it's dead good.'

'Dead good,' murmured Cat and wrote that down.

Tom struggled to change the subject. He waved a hand at the rows of tiny soldiers standing in neatly ordered ranks. There must have been hundreds of them, all more or less identical. There were also little pots of paint, brushes, what looked like a collection of carving knives and some blocks of wood. 'What's with all the toy soldiers?' he asked.

Fraser looked rather indignant at this description. 'They're not toys,' he said. 'They're models. It's a hobby of mine. I carve them.'

'Wow. What, *all* of them?'

'Not quite all.' Fraser indicated a section of perhaps twenty or so tiny soldiers to his left, standing proudly to attention; each of them carrying a tiny wooden gun. They looked a little more knocked about than their companions, the paint scratched and weathered as if by the passing of time. 'These wee fellows belonged to my great grandfather, Angus. They were sent with his belongings from Culloden and handed down to me.'

'Culloden.' Tom frowned. 'I don't think I know that. Is it near Edinburgh?'

Catriona giggled. 'He means the *battle* of Culloden, silly! Great grandfather Angus was a Jacobite.'

'Was he?' Tom tried to look impressed, but would have been the first to admit that his knowledge of Scottish history was scant to say the least. 'Is that like a . . . vegetarian thing?'

Now Fraser looked horrified. 'The Jacobites supported Charles Stuart,' he said. 'They wanted to put him back on the throne of England. I should have thought you'd know that.'

'Oh yeah,' said Tom. 'That's right, I remember now.' He didn't really, but it seemed like the best thing to say.

Fraser pointed to a larger section of tiny troops. 'These ones I've carved and painted myself,' he said with evident pride. 'It's interesting that you said you're from Manchester. A small number of troops that fought at Culloden on the Jacobite side were actually from a Manchester regiment.'

'No way!' said Tom, and noticed Cat wrote that down

as well. He frowned, wondering what a future historian would make of the notebook if it were ever discovered. He pointed to a jumbled pile of little wooden figures at one end of the table, through which Jamie was now rooting eagerly.

'What about these guys?' he asked.

'Them?' Fraser looked rather less pleased with himself. 'They're just discards,' he said. 'Ones that didn't turn out quite right.' He lifted the hooked knife. 'This is really a cobbler's knife. Sometimes it slips and an arm comes off. Then you have to start all over again. I hate it when that happens.'

As Tom watched, Jamie picked up a tiny wooden figure from the pile. It was dressed in a crudely-made checked pattern suit. Tom experienced a sudden rush of recognition. He'd seen that figure before, perhaps only half an hour ago, stretched out in a little wooden coffin in the National Museum of Scotland. He couldn't suppress a gasp of astonishment.

'Wh . . . what's the matter?' asked Jamie.

'Er . . . it's just that one you're holding,' said Tom, pointing. 'He's . . . not wearing a . . . proper uniform.'

'No, I made him that wee suit,' said Cat gleefully. 'I felt sorry for him.' She glanced critically at her brother. 'I wanted to make dresses for some of the others but Fraser wouldn't allow it.'

'I should think not!' said Fraser. 'They're *soldiers*. What do you suppose great grandfather would say if he heard about such a thing?'

'He's still around is he?' asked Tom.

'No, of course he's not around! He died at Culloden in 1746, massacred by the Duke of Cumberland along with the rest of his regiment.' He looked at Tom warily. 'You'll have heard of Cumberland, I suppose?'

'Er . . . yeah, is he the one who made the sausages?'

Jamie laughed. 'He c . . . c . . . certainly made sausages out of the J . . . Jacobites!' he said and Fraser gave him a stern look.

'That's no' funny,' he said.

'Oh, come along, Fraser, it *was* a long time ago,' said Cat. 'You carry on as though it only happened yesterday.' She looked at Tom. 'You'll have to forgive him. He's a wee bit obsessed with Culloden. I keep saying he's made enough soldiers now and he should turn his skills to something new. But will he listen? Oh, no.' She studied Tom for a moment. 'So, what brings you to Edinburgh?'

'The Virgin Pendolino,' said Tom, without thinking and saw the girl's eyebrows arch at his words. 'Oh, that's just a . . . a train,' he said.

'A train? You mean, like a . . . railway train?'

'Yeah, you know . . . I suppose yours are a bit different. Steam trains? Chuff chuffs?' He made a few circular motions with his arms.

Fraser nodded. 'I didn't realise you could come so far by train,' he said. 'Slow, noisy things. A friend of mine went to Perth on one, but it took him hours and his clothes were all full of soot by the time he got there.'

'Our trains are different. Quicker . . . well, most of the time anyway.'

'Still, that's a . . . t . . . terrible distance,' observed Jaimie. 'How long did it take to get here?'

'Oh, hours,' said Tom; and then, seeing their reactions, realised he must have got it wrong again. 'A whole load of hours. Days worth of them, in fact. Yeah, now I think about it, it must have taken one . . . two, maybe three days?'

They looked impressed. 'The world's a smaller place,' observed Cat. 'Imagine such speed.'

Tom wondered what they'd think if he told them the truth. The train he'd taken had got him from Manchester Piccadilly to Edinburgh Waverley station in a cool three hours and fifteen minutes.

'I'd love to visit England,' said Cat wistfully. 'The furthest we've ever travelled is to Glasgow and that was for a funeral. What's the furthest you've ever travelled Tom?'

Good question. Tom considered offering an answer of 'three hundred and sixty years' but decided against it.

'Tom's l . . . looking for somewhere to s . . . stay,' said Jamie.

'Well he can't stay here,' said Fraser, bluntly.

Cat looked at him. 'Fraser, don't be rude!'

'I'm not being rude. We haven't the room. And even if we had, you know Da wouldn't allow it.' He looked at Tom. 'Da is very strict. We daren't even tell him that

Jamie comes here sometimes. He wouldnae approve.'

'What does your dad do?' asked Tom.

'Oh, he's a saw maker,' said Cat. 'It's quite skilled work and everyone says he's the best in Edinburgh. But he doesn't know that Jamie comes here and that we feed him sometimes. It's a wee secret.'

'Right.' Tom looked thoughtfully at the pile of discards on the table. 'Do you guys ever get up to Arthur's Seat?' he asked.

'Sometimes in the summer,' said Cat. 'When the weather's nice, we take a picnic up there. Why do you ask?'

'Oh, I just . . . wondered if you ever went there. And . . . did you ever think about making little coffins for these leftover soldiers?'

Fraser gave him a disapproving look. 'What an odd idea,' he said. 'Why would I want to do a thing like that?'

Just then they heard Mary calling from downstairs.

'Supper,' said Cat, closing her notebook. 'Come along, Tom. Let's see what we've got to eat today.'

And they made their way downstairs.

Five

It was a simple meal. A wooden table in the cramped kitchen had been set for five. There were thick slices of homemade bread, butter and a big black pan of what looked like vegetable stew. Tom was very hungry now and grateful for whatever he was offered. They took their seats and watched as Mary ladled helpings of the thick, steaming stew into earthenware bowls. Tom reached eagerly for his spoon and was about to make a start when he realised that everybody had bowed their heads and were looking at their bowls in silence, so he set the spoon down again.

'Perhaps our guest would be kind enough to say grace?' suggested Mary.

'Yes, let's have a Manchester prayer!' said Cat, excitedly.

Tom thought for a moment. He wasn't the world's biggest churchgoer so he guessed he'd just have to improvise. 'Umm . . . right,' he said. 'Sure. No problem. Er . . . thanks, oh Lord, for giving us this scran, which is . . . just exactly what the doctor ordered.' There was an uncomfortable silence, so he added, 'That's it. We always keep it short in Manchester. So the . . . food doesn't get cold.'

'Amen,' said everybody and reached for the spoons.

'Tom was just telling us he came here by coach,'

said Cat, buttering a slice of bread. 'It only took him three days to get here.'

'Gracious,' said Mary. 'You came here with your parents, did you?'

'Er . . . no,' said Tom. 'No, my dad put me on the tr . . . on the coach.'

'You travelled alone?' Mary seemed surprised. 'Forgive me, but those highways are lawless places. Aren't you a little young to be off on your own?'

'Not really,' said Tom. He took a mouthful of hot stew, which had a coarse, earthy flavour, but he'd eaten much worse on his last visit. 'No, I'm used to it.'

'And you have relatives here in Edinburgh?'

'No, I . . . I'm all alone,' admitted Tom. 'I was supposed to be staying with my mum, but . . . well, I'm not sure what's happened to her.'

'He's l . . . looking for a place to stay,' said Jamie. 'I said I'd t . . . try and help him. I thought m . . . maybe you might have some ideas.'

'Goodness. That *is* a tall order.' Mary thought for a moment. 'What exactly has happened to your mother?'

'I've kind of lost her. That happens sometimes. But I'm sure she'll show up sooner or later. She usually does.'

'Perhaps Tom should go to the constables,' suggested Fraser. 'Maybe they could help him find her?'

'Oh, there's no need for that,' said Tom, hastily. 'No, she'll turn up. I just need somewhere to wait around for a while until she does.'

'There *is* a lodging house on Tanner's Close,' admitted Mary. 'Though I'm not sure it's a suitable place for a young lad on his own.'

'Oh, yes,' said Jamie, excitedly. 'I'd f . . . forgotten about that. I know somebody who l . . . lodges there! My friend B . . . Billy. I b . . . bet he'd keep an eye on you until your ma turns up.'

'Billy?' Tom looked at him. 'Who's Billy?'

'Just a fellow I know,' said Jamie. 'Irish Billy, they call him. He's a good sort. We'll g . . . go and see him after we've eaten. You s . . . said you've got money, didn't you?'

Tom nodded. 'English money.'

'Oh, I'm sure they'll take any manner of currency in *that* place,' said Mary. She sounded as though she didn't really approve. 'But you mark my words, Tom. You want to be careful out on those streets. There's all kinds of rum things going on, out there. People being robbed . . . and worse.'

'People disappearing,' said Cat, in a melodramatic whisper.

'Wheesht,' said Mary.

'It's true,' Cat assured her. She looked at Tom. 'People are saying there's a killer on the loose.'

'Catriona!' said Mary. 'You'll frighten the boy. Hasn't he just told us his own poor mother is missing?'

'Oh, no, not like that,' Tom assured her. 'I mean, I know that's how it sounded, but . . . well, I'm not worried about anything happening to her *here*.' He looked at Cat. 'People disappearing?' he prompted her.

'I'm only saying what I've heard,' insisted Cat. 'And you have to admit, Mama, something strange *is* going on.'

Mary gave Tom an encouraging smile. 'There was an old lady called Effie,' she said. 'Pathetic thing, she was, used to go around trying to sell scraps of leather to earn a few pennies, you'd see her on the close most days of the week. Then suddenly, one day, she was gone. Nobody knows what happened to her. Seems to have just vanished into thin air.'

Fraser smirked. 'She was fond of the gin,' he said. 'Probably drank herself to death.'

'I don't know where you came by that information, Fraser McCallum, but I'd thank you not to be spreading gossip,' said Mary. 'In this house we speak well of people or we don't say anything at all.'

Fraser scowled. 'It's what everyone else is saying,' he muttered. He dipped a hunk of bread into his bowl of stew and took a big bite. 'Charlie Buchanan told me that she . . .'

'Don't speak with your mouth full,' Mary chided him. 'Charlie Buchanan! She thought for a moment. 'Isn't he the one who claimed that he had an imp in a bottle who could grant any wish in return for a penny? And correct me if I'm wrong, Fraser, but aren't you one of the boys who fell for that nonsense?'

Fraser reddened. 'To be fair, I was only little at the time,' he said.

'Nevertheless, I would have thought it might serve as a warning to you to disregard anything that boy has to say.' She sighed. 'Effie was just a poor lost soul and her only crime was that she grew old, with no family to care for her. She's not the only person to go missing either. All through the year, there've been people . . . the old, the weak, the homeless . . .'

'Mama!' said Cat sternly. '*Tom's* homeless.'

There was a brief silence while they all considered her words.

'I wish he could stay with *us*,' added Cat, wistfully.

'You know he can't,' said Mary. She looked at Tom. 'I'm sorry. I'd love to be able to say that we could put you up for a while, but . . .'

'Yeah, I know,' said Tom. 'Mr McCallum wouldn't like it.'

'Ach, it's not that he's a mean man, you understand, but he came from a very poor family and he watches every penny. And of course, with the children's education and everything, money is rather tight. If he even knew that Jamie ate here from time to time, he'd be far from happy.' She glanced at Jamie. 'Especially since he knows that Jamie has a loving mother not so very far from here.'

Jamie grimaced. 'If she l . . . loves me, she's a funny way of showing it! That one's far too f . . . fond of beating out a rhythm on my b . . . backside.'

'I dare say you've pushed her into doing it,' said Mary. 'You'd try the patience of St Andrew himself,

Jamie Wilson!' She turned back to Tom. 'So you see, I'm afraid I can't offer you a place to stay, much as I'd like to.'

'Don't sweat it,' said Tom.

'I beg your pardon, my dear?'

'That'll be a Manchester expression,' said Cat, knowingly. 'Tom's teaching me them.' She lowered her voice to a gruff approximation of Tom's accent. 'I wooden 'old yer breaf,' she said and smiled proudly.

'I reckon Tom's made a b . . . big impression on Catriona,' observed Jamie.

'It's *Cat*,' she reminded him. She looked at her Mother. 'It's what they'd call me in Manchester.'

'Is it now?' Mary smiled. 'I'd say it suits you. I've always thought there's something of the feline about you, with those green eyes.'

'What would Ma's name be shortened to?' wondered Cat.

'I've an Auntie Mary back home,' said Tom. 'Everyone calls her Mae.'

Mary smiled. 'Yes, I've heard that used. And Mollie, too, of course.'

'That's actually longer,' observed Fraser. 'What's the point of a shortened name that has more letters in it?'

It was a good question, which nobody seemed to have an answer for.

Mary looked at Tom. 'With regard to the lodging house, Tom, you must do as you think best until your

50

mother arrives. But I'd be grateful if you'd call here from time to time. In the day. Just to let us know that everything's all right with you and perhaps to have a wee bite to eat.'

Tom smiled. He felt touched by her concern, a woman he'd only met a little while ago. 'I'll be fine,' he assured her. 'Really.'

'But you *will* call in?'

'Yes,' Cat urged him. 'You must. I need to learn more Manchester-talk.' She indicated Tom's T Shirt. 'Mama, have you ever seen anything like that before?'

'I must confess I haven't,' said Mary. 'Is that what they wear in England, these days?'

'Er . . . not everyone,' said Tom.

'It's dead cool,' said Cat, and Tom nearly choked on a piece of bread.

'What?' asked Cat. 'Did I say it wrong?'

'Er . . . no,' spluttered Tom. 'No, that's . . . perfect.' How could he tell her that it just seemed so weird coming from the lips of someone in the nineteenth century? He smiled at Cat. He was somewhat alarmed to note that he rather liked looking into her lovely green eyes. 'You're coming on a treat,' he told her. 'We'll soon have you talking like a proper Manc.'

'I don't know what Professor Robertson would say if he heard you using words like that,' said Mary.

'He's my tutor from the University,' explained Cat. 'And I think he'd be pleased. He told me that if you want to be a writer, you have to spread your net wide . . . take in as many life experiences as you can. Who knows? One day I might want to set a story in Manchester.'

Fraser shook his head. 'I keep telling you, sister, girls like you don't stand a chance of becoming writers.'

'Nonsense! What about Jane Austen? She was a woman and she published novels. And what about Mary Brunton? She's from right here in Edinburgh.'

'Aye, and she wasnae raised in a wee house on Tanner's Close, neither. You have to be a member of the gentry to get anywhere in *that* world.'

'It shouldn't matter where you come from,' argued Cat. 'My words are as valuable as anybody's.' She looked to Tom. 'Jane Austen was an English writer. Are there other women who are published in England?'

Tom shrugged his shoulders. 'Some,' he admitted as through his head rampaged a series of female writers. J.K. Rowling, Jacqueline Wilson, Enid Blyton . . . Of course, he could hardly mention them, since they didn't actually exist yet. 'You should stick to your guns, Cat,' he said. 'There might not be all that many of you now, but trust me, there *will* be. One day, there'll be lots of women writers.'

Cat beamed at him, an act that made Tom feel strangely warm inside. Then she turned to her brother and stuck her tongue out at him.

'Stop it, Catriona,' said Mary. 'The wind will change and you'll be stuck like that forever.'

They finished up the meal, mopping out their bowls

with their last crusts of bread and then Mary made a big pot of tea and they sat around the table, chatting and laughing until Mary glanced at the clock on the wall and announced that her husband would be arriving back from work soon. Tom took this as an indication that it was time to leave and sure enough, Jamie stood up from the table and motioned towards the door.

'We'd b . . . best get moving if we're to s . . . sort you out a place for the night,' he said. Tom nodded. He said goodbye to everyone and followed Jamie out to the hallway, but Cat insisted on walking out with him. Jamie opened the door to the street and stepped outside. Tom was surprised to see that it was already getting dark out there, the sun sinking below the roofs of the surrounding tenements. Tom hesitated a moment and turned back at the doorway to look at Cat.

'It's been nice to meet you,' he said and he reached out to shake her hand.

'It's been dead cool,' she told him, leaning forward impulsively and kissing him on the cheek. He stood, aware that he was reddening, but he couldn't deny how good it had felt. 'Now don't forget,' she urged him. 'You're to call back soon and tell us how you're getting on.'

'I will,' he assured her. He turned away and stepped out onto the street, pulling the door closed behind him. Jamie was waiting for him with a knowing smile on his face.

'I don't w . . . want to hurry you,' he said.

'Oh, that's ok.'

'D . . . didn't I tell you the McCallums were a n . . . n . . . nice family?'

'You did,' admitted Tom. 'And they are.'

'Particularly C . . . C . . . Catriona?' observed Jamie.

'It's Cat,' Tom corrected him. They headed off along the darkening street and despite the gathering chill of evening, Tom felt a warm glow that stayed with him for quite a distance.

Six

'This is the p . . . p . . . place,' announced Jamie.

Tom had to admit that it didn't look very promising – a shabby, tumbledown building of grey stone, rearing up on the crowded side street ahead of them and surrounded on all sides by other equally shabby dwellings. Three steps led up to a ramshackle door affixed to a kind of porch on the side of the building and it was impossible to get an idea of how big the place actually was inside. Above the door, a crudely-made painted sign announced that this was *Laird's Lodging House: Proprietor Mrs M. Laird.*

Jamie climbed the steps and hammered on the wooden door with his fist, the sound seemed to reverberate throughout the whole building. They waited in silence for a moment and then the door creaked open and a woman peered out at them, a heavyset middle aged woman wearing an odd frilly bonnet that did nothing to soften the severity of her features. She had dark, piercing eyes, emphasised by thin black brows and the expression on her face suggested that she had just encountered a bad smell. She took in Jamie at a glance and then her steely gaze flicked across to Tom. Her eyebrows arched in surprise and Tom reminded himself that this was probably because his clothes looked so out of place. Her mouth twisted into a sneer and she turned her unwelcoming stare back to Jamie.

'What do you want?' she growled, making no attempt at a smile. 'If you're selling something, we don't want it and if you've come to beg, you'll be sorely disappointed.' She had an Irish accent. Northern Irish, Tom thought, though he was no expert.

Jamie tried to smile. 'H . . . hello Margaret,' he said. 'H . . . how are you today?'

'Never mind the pleasantries! I asked you what you wanted.'

'Er . . . I was j . . . just wondering if I could speak to B . . . B . . . Billy,' said Jamie. 'If he's around.'

The woman looked annoyed. 'Oh aye, he's *around*, all right,' she admitted. 'Laying around, talking the hind legs off anyone who'll listen. What's this concerning?'

'Er . . . I'd . . . r . . . rather talk to Billy,' insisted Jamie.

Margaret scowled, as though considering throwing him down the steps. 'Oh, very well,' she said at last. 'I'll go and see if he wants to speak to you.' Jamie made to take a step into the building, but she placed a meaty hand on his chest, stopping him in his tracks. 'You wait here,' she said and slammed the door in his face.

There was a brief silence.

'She seems a charmer,' observed Tom. 'Who is she?'

'The l . . . l . . . landlady,' said Jamie, forlornly. 'Mrs Laird. I'm afraid she's a bit of a r . . . r . . .'

'Rat Bag?' suggested Tom.

'I was g . . . going to say, 'rum character,'' said Jamie. 'But I think your description is b . . . b . . . better!'

'Are you sure you don't know somewhere else I could stay?' asked Tom, hopefully. If Margaret was any measure of the welcome he might expect here, it didn't seem like he'd have an agreeable stay. 'Is there like maybe a Travelodge or something?'

Just then the door opened a second time and a man stood there, a stocky young fellow with fair hair that came down the sides of his ruddy face in two elaborate sideburns. He wore a white shirt, buttoned at the neck with a fancy-looking black bow tie, and a green velvet waistcoat. When he saw Jamie, his face split into an amiable grin, revealing rows of even white teeth.

'Well, now,' he exclaimed. 'As I live and breathe, if it isn't Master Jamie!' His accent was much like Mrs Laird's, hard and guttural and Tom remembered that Jamie had referred to him as 'Irish' Billy. The man was holding a white clay pipe in one hand and he took a moment to lift it to his lips in order to take a couple of leisurely puffs from it. 'What brings you to our door?' he asked.

Jamie indicated Tom. 'This is my English friend, T . . . Tom Afflick. He's just arrived here in Edinburgh and he has n . . . nowhere to stay. We wondered if there might b . . . be a room here for him.'

'I have money,' said Tom quickly.

Billy studied him with evident interest, taking in his unusual clothing.

'An Englishman, is it?' He puffed on the pipe again, sending fragrant wafts of smoke up into the air. 'I'd say fashions have changed a bit since I was last there.' He studied the lettering on Tom's t-shirt for a moment, as though trying to puzzle it out. 'You have some family with you, Tom?' he asked. 'Parents . . . brothers or sisters?'

'No, sir, it's just me,' said Tom.

Billy looked unconvinced. 'What, a bright young feller like you?' he cried. 'You surely must have *some* relatives around the city.'

'Uh uh.' Tom shook his head. 'I used to know people on Mary King's Close . . . but that was . . . er, years ago.'

'So what you're telling me is you're an orphan?'

'Er . . . kind of.' It seemed to Tom that it was easier to go along with this than to try and explain the actual situation. For one thing, it was complicated. For another, Billy would probably decide he was some kind of escaped lunatic. He reached into his pocket. 'Like I was saying, I can pay you . . .'

Billy put out a hand to stop Tom. 'I wouldn't even think about taking your money!' he announced grandly. 'Why, I couldn't live with meself if I did a thing like that. A man has his pride, you know, and I reckon William will say just the same.'

'William?' asked Tom.

'He's the l . . . l . . . landlord,' explained Jamie.

'Aye, that's right,' agreed Billy, with a sly wink. 'Billy and Will, we are. And would you believe the two of us boyos are from pretty much the same part of the auld country, but only met here in Edinburgh a year ago? That's fate, that is, no two ways about it.' He leaned closer to confide a secret. 'Margaret won't be keen on the idea of you staying, you can bet your boots on that, but you just leave it to me to sweet talk William and I reckon you'll have a place to lay your head before you even know it. Tell you what, why don't you wait here, while I go and have a quick word with 'em?'

'Er . . . ok,' said Tom doubtfully and for a second time, the door was closed in their faces. Tom stood there shivering. Now the sun had gone down, the temperature was rapidly falling. He wasn't even sure he liked the look of the boarding house, but he was in no position to be choosy and he knew he didn't want to spend the night sleeping rough on the streets, even if Jamie claimed to know some 'good places'.

'So how do you know this Billy?' he asked Jamie.

'Oh, just from around,' said Jamie. 'He's always b . . . been kind to me. Gives me money to get food sometimes. Once he paid me two pennies to r . . . run an errand for him.'

'What kind of errand?'

'A d . . . d . . . delivery,' said Jamie. 'Me and another fellow, John, we h . . . had to take a tea chest up to the S . . . Surgeons' Hall in the city. We pushed it along on a trolley. A man met us there and t . . . took the tea chest inside. Then he came out and p . . . paid us ten pounds!'

Tom tried to look suitably impressed. While it didn't sound very much, he was well aware from Jamie's excited expression that this must be big money.

'What was in the tea chest?' he asked.

Jamie shrugged. 'I don't know,' he said.

'Weren't you curious? I mean, you could have had a peek inside, surely?'

Jamie shook his head. 'It was nailed shut,' he said. 'Anyway, we bought the ten pounds back to B . . . Billy and he gave us another tuppence each for our t . . . troubles. That was a good night's work, I can tell you! I bought a b . . . big chocolate cake and I ate the lot!'

'But didn't you ask . . .?'

At that moment, the door opened again and there was Billy, grinning out at them and looking very pleased with himself.

'It's all arranged, so ' he announced. 'We've a place for you to lay your head and we've even had a thought about a few wee jobs you could do around the house, to help earn your keep.'

This didn't sound like the best news to Tom. He thought about some of the horrific things he'd been made to do back in the seventeenth century, one of which had been to act as apprentice to a bogus plague doctor. He considered putting up some kind of protest, but now one of Billy's big hands was on his shoulder, drawing him inside, and for the moment there seemed to be no real option but to go along with things. He paused on the step and glanced uncertainly at Jamie. 'What about you?' he said.

'I'll b . . . be on my way,' said Jamie. 'I n . . . need to find my own place for the n . . . n . . . night.'

'Oh, but . . .' Tom looked at Billy. 'Isn't there somewhere for Jamie to stay?' he pleaded. While sleeping on the streets wasn't an appealing proposition, neither did he much like the idea of being left alone in this grim-looking place.

Billy looked at Tom, seemingly puzzled by the suggestion. Then he glanced at Jamie as though he'd actually forgotten he was there. He shook his head. 'I'm afraid we've only room for the one,' he said. 'But Jamie is well used to looking after himself, I'd say.' He registered Tom's look of disappointment and reaching into the pocket of his waistcoat, he took out a coin which he pressed into Jamie's hand. 'There's a penny for you, young feller-me-lad,' he said. 'You make sure you get a cup of something hot inside you before you turn in for the night.'

'Thank you, Billy,' said Jamie. He looked at Tom. 'I'll d . . . drop by tomorrow,' he suggested. 'S . . . see how you're getting on.'

'Ok,' said Tom. 'That'll be cool.' He was going to add something else, but now Billy had a brawny arm around his shoulders and was drawing him into the gloom. Tom caught just a glimpse of Jamie's pale face peering in at him and then the door slammed shut yet again and Billy was leading him along a narrow hallway that smelled of raw meat and boiled cabbage.

'Step right this way,' he said, in a jovial voice. 'And I'll introduce you to the rest of the merry crew!'

Seven

They entered a large, dimly-lit room. Heavy curtains covered the windows, drawn tight against the outside world as though it was not welcome in there. To Tom's left there was a crudely-made wooden counter which ran the whole length of the room. Behind it, rows of large wooden barrels lay on their sides, stacked on stout shelves and wedged firmly in place. The counter top was covered in scores of clay and metal tankards.

Margaret skulked behind the counter, regarding Tom sullenly as though she still didn't want him to be here. He noticed that she now had a tiny baby clutched under one arm. It was swathed in layers of blanket and howling pitifully although Margaret wasn't taking any notice of it. Every so often its crying was interrupted by a bout of violent coughing, though that didn't merit Margaret's attention either. She carried it as though it had no more importance than a bundle of dirty washing.

At the far end of the room customers sat around smaller tables, drinking from tankards, playing cards or watching a grey-haired old man who was standing on a slightly raised stage and playing a fiddle, badly, producing sounds that resembled the noises made by cats on hot summer nights. Over everything hung a fog of smoke and body odour and the thick, acrid stench of stale beer.

'Here we are,' said Billy, proudly. 'The finest drinking den in Edinburgh!'

He drew Tom towards a larger pine table to their right, where a man and a young woman were sitting with drinks in front of them. The woman glanced up at Tom and smiled welcomingly. A tangle of dark curls framed her face which, despite being whitened with powder, still looked bewitchingly pretty. Her blue eyes were outlined with black and her full lips painted a deep red.

'Well, who have we here?' she asked.

'This is Tom,' said Billy, pushing him down into a chair beside her. 'From England,' he added, as though this was important. 'Tom, this lovely lady is Nell McDougall and I don't mind telling you she's my sweetheart, so I'll thank you to keep your hands off her.' He chortled merrily and Nell laughed along with him.

'Er . . . hi,' said Tom, awkwardly, aware that his face was reddening. 'Don't worry, I wouldn't . . . I mean, I'm not . . .'

'Ach, ignore him,' said Nell. 'He just likes putting people on the spot.' She had a Scottish accent, Tom thought, but not the genteel tones of Edinburgh. She sounded coarser, harder, somehow. Glasgow, perhaps? 'And besides,' she added with a sly wink, 'Billy knows I always have an eye for a handsome young feller.'

Now Tom felt himself blushing to his roots, but Billy continued talking as though nothing had happened.

'And *this* fine gentleman is Will, who I was already telling you about.'

Tom turned his head to take in the man at the table and immediately felt a stab of distrust. He was tall and skinny, with jet-black hair pulled back from his forehead and greased down onto his skull like a cap. He had a sharp, hawk-like nose and his long, thin face seemed permanently fixed in a sardonic grin. Most discomforting though, were his eyes which seemed to smoulder with a fierce intensity. When he spoke his accent was much like Billy's.

'I'm told yer an orphan,' he said.

Tom didn't feel in any position to argue the case. 'Er . . . yeah,' he said. 'It sucks.'

Billy and Will exchanged a puzzled look, but the grin soon etched itself back onto Will's face. 'Well, you've come to the right place,' he said. 'We take all sorts in here, don't we, Billy?'

'We do,' agreed Billy, sitting down and reaching for a half-filled tankard on the table. He took a generous swallow. 'All kinds of waifs and strays and sure, don't we look after 'em well? Don't we treat 'em like they was our very own kith and kin?' He sniggered and Tom noticed that Nell shot him a challenging look.

'The boy must be thirsty,' she said. 'And hungry, I shouldn't wonder.'

'Oh, no, I just ate,' Tom assured them. 'I wouldn't mind a drink though.'

'You *ate*?' Billy scowled. 'Where, exactly?'

64

'At the McCallums, just up the road.'

'But . . . weren't you just after telling me that you didn't know anybody in Edinburgh?'

Tom shrugged. 'Jamie took me there. *He* knows them.'

'The McCallums from Tanner's Close?' muttered Will.

'Yeah. Is that a problem?'

'Er . . . no, no,' said Billy, waving a hand. 'I was just surprised, that's all. You being a stranger here and everyt'ing.' Tom could see that Will was glaring accusingly at Billy, but Billy was doing his best to ignore it. 'So, what drink will it be, Tom?' he asked. 'Ale or whisky?'

'Umm . . . any chance of a diet coke?' asked Tom without thinking. And then added quickly, 'Or maybe just a glass of water?'

This seemed to amuse Billy. 'I wouldn't drink the water here if I was you,' he said. 'The last man who tried *that* is pushing up the daisies in Greyfriars!' He laughed at his own joke, then turned his head to the bar and waved a hand. 'Margaret, my dear, I wonder if you'd be so kind as to bring young Tom here a tankard of your finest ale?'

Margaret shot a look of pure vitriol across the counter, but she picked up a clay tankard with her free hand and began to fill it from one of the barrels. The baby carried on with its shrieking and coughing.

'I don't think Margaret likes me,' muttered Tom.

'Of course she likes you,' said Billy, taking another gulp from his drink. 'Sure, that's just her way. She's what you call a diamond in the rough.'

'She's what I call a rat bag,' said Tom, and heard a sharp intake of breath from Nell. He looked at her. 'Oh, sorry,' he said. 'Is she a friend of yours?'

He saw that both Nell and Billy were now looking anxiously at Will, as though expecting him to say something, but the thin man's expression remained unchanged, the same insincere grin that was more of a grimace than anything else.

'Margaret is what you call highly-strung,' he said. 'You get used to her.'

'Will is married to Margaret,' explained Nell.

'Not properly married,' added Billy. 'Common-law, I think they call it. But it's as good as.' He winked at Nell. 'It's good enough for us two, anyway!'

Tom began to wish that he had a spade so he could dig a hole, climb in and cover himself with earth. He looked helplessly at Will. 'Erm . . . Mr Laird, in . . . in Manchester, that word, rat bag, it means that you're sort of . . .'

'I well know what the word means,' said Will. 'And the name's not Laird, neither. Wasn't Billy just after telling you that it's a common-law arrangement?' At that moment Margaret arrived with the tankard of ale in one hand and the screaming baby still tucked under her other arm. She slammed the drink down so hard in front of Tom that some of the contents actually slopped out and splashed his face.

'Er . . . thanks,' he said.

'You are most welcome,' growled Margaret and stalked back to her place at the bar, taking her clamouring baby with her. As they departed, the child emitted another bout of hacking coughs, which, this time, degenerated into a series of ragged howling sounds.

'That baby,' said Tom. 'It doesn't sound well.'

Everybody nodded.

'She has the whooping cough,' said Nell. 'It's a terrible thing.'

'Has she seen a doctor?' asked Tom.

This seemed to amuse Billy and Will.

'Doctors,' said Will. 'Quacks, the lot of 'em.'

'Though of course, they *do* have their uses,' said Billy.

'I'll drink to that,' said Will and raised his tankard. The two men drank and Billy motioned to Tom to join them. He lifted the heavy tankard to his lips. The dark liquid smelled like stagnant pond water and didn't taste a whole lot better, but Tom forced himself to swallow down a mouthful, if only to keep the peace. Billy and Will seemed to be enjoying some kind of private joke and Tom told himself that there was something decidedly dodgy about them, though he had to confess that Billy seemed the more likable of the two. By a long shot.

'So you're a friend of Jamie's?' said Nell.

Tom nodded and gratefully set down the tankard.

'Well, yeah . . . though I only met him a couple of hours ago. He seems really nice.'

'Oh, surely,' agreed Nell. 'Everyone knows Jamie.'

'That's just the problem,' said Billy, and Will smirked as though he'd said something funny.

'What do you mean?' asked Tom.

'Aww, nothin' really,' said Billy. 'He's a nice enough young feller. It's just that sometimes it doesn't pay for your face to be too familiar. We're big supporters of new faces around here, aren't we Will?

'We are,' agreed Will.

' Now then, Tom. Me and Will had us a little talk and we decided you might like to take on a few jobs here. To earn your keep, so to speak.'

Tom shrugged. He didn't much like the sound of this. 'What kind of jobs?'

'Oh, collecting tankards, sweeping the floor, stuff like that.'

Tom cast an eye around the place. It didn't look as though it had ever been cleaned in its entire history. 'Er . . . sure, why not?' he said. He told himself that with any luck he wouldn't be around long enough to actually *do* much work. 'Will I be paid for it?'

Billy and Will looked at each other and burst out laughing. Tom looked from one to the other in dismay. He wasn't aware that he had said something funny.

Eventually, Billy calmed down enough to reply. 'We thought board and lodging would be ample payment,' he said. 'Most other people have to pay rent to stay here.'

'Oh, sure. I only wondered,' said Tom. 'And I know you paid Jamie to make that delivery, so . . .'

Billy and Will regarded Tom in silence for a moment.

'What do you know about that?' asked Will and the grin had finally disappeared from his face.

'Oh, er . . . only what Jamie told me. He said you wanted a tea chest taken around to . . . the Surgeons' Hall, was it? And that you were paid ten pounds for what was inside it.'

Will glared at Billy. 'I told you that boy was a blabbermouth,' he said.

Billy laughed unconvincingly. 'Ah, nobody pays any mind to *him*. They all think he's gone in the head.'

'Oh, Jamie's not stupid,' Tom assured them. 'I thought that when I first met him, but then he showed me that trick with the snuffbox? You know what? I think he might be autistic.'

'Oh, yes, he is,' said Nell. 'He drew a picture of me once, it was very good.'

'No, not artistic. *Aut*istic.' He looked around the table and received nothing but blank looks in return. Clearly the term was more modern than he had imagined. 'He's . . . not what you think,' he said at last. 'He's . . . clever.'

Will frowned. 'Maybe too clever for his own good,' he murmured.

'Ah, relax,' said Billy. He looked at Tom. 'I can see you're a clever lad, Tom, so I'll level with yer. What it is, we supply the surgeons with meat for their kitchens, so we do. We have a trusted supplier and we get them some choice cuts at a bit of a discount. But it's . . .

not done through the books, if you know what I mean? There's strict laws governing the movement of beef in this city. That's why we always take the stuff round there at night. So, I'd appreciate it if you'd keep that quiet, all right?'

Tom nodded. 'Ok,' he said. 'Whatever.'

'Good lad.' Billy glanced at Will and smiled, then changed the subject. 'Well, come on, this is no fun at all! We'll have another drink, so.' He turned and waved to Margaret. 'Bring us another round, Margaret, my dear,' he said. 'Whiskies this time.'

'You'll show me the colour of your money first,' said Margaret uncharitably.

'Ah, serve 'em,' growled Will. 'I know they're good for it.'

'No more for me!' said Tom, hastily. 'Really.'

Billy shrugged. 'Suit yourself,' he said. 'Just the three of us, then.'

Margaret seemed far from pleased, but she set down the baby in a corner, filled three glasses and brought them over on a tray which she slammed down with more force than necessary.

Nell glared up at her. 'Have you got something to say to me?' she snarled.

'What would I have to say to the likes of you?' replied Margaret, glaring back at her. The two women stared at each other in silence for a moment before Margaret turned on her heel and flounced back to the bar.

Nell grinned ruefully at Tom. 'See, it's not just you,' she said.

'Ah, ignore her,' suggested Will. 'She's in one of her moods. Come on, let's drink.' He raised his glass of whisky. 'To free enterprise!' he said and knocked it back in one gulp.

The rest of the evening dissolved into a drinking session. Tom got through it by politely sipping at his foul-tasting ale, while Billy and Will got progressively drunker. At one point a woman at the top end of the room got up to sing along to the man with the fiddle, some nonsense about when she 'walked out one fine summer's morning.' The woman had a screeching, toneless voice, which only made the resulting noise even more unbearable. Billy and Will sat there making rude comments about the woman's singing and laughing uproariously at their own jokes. Tom began to feel tired and, although he had only sipped at the ale, a little woozy. He wondered if he could politely slip away, but luckily Nell seemed to notice his predicament. She leaned closer.

'You want me to show you where you'll be sleeping?' she asked him.

He nodded gratefully and she got up from the table and led Tom up to the far end of the room. As they went past the bar he was aware of Margaret, looking daggers at them. Nell ignored her and led him through a door at the side of the room, along a hallway, out through a back entrance and across a cold yard. Tom glanced up at the sky and saw that it was now pitch black, glittering with handfuls of stars. Ahead of them lay what looked like the open doorway of a stable, a long, low building with a thatched roof. At the entrance Nell paused to light an oil lamp which stood on a barrel beside the door. She lifted the lantern and led the way inside.

Sure enough, it was a stable. Tom's nostrils were assailed by the powerful smell of pigs, something all too familiar to him from his last visit into the past. He could hear the sounds of them grunting and snuffling on the other side of a wooden partition. But Nell led him to an empty stall, spread with a thick layer of what looked like clean straw. She set the lantern carefully down on a barrel. She was quite drunk, Tom thought, swaying slightly on her feet. She indicated a rusty bucket standing in one corner.

'That's for if you have to make water,' she explained.

'If I have to . . .? Oh er . . . thanks,' said Tom, embarrassed. He looked forlornly around.

'I know it's not much, but if you snuggle down deep into that straw, you should be warm enough, I reckon.'

Tom nodded. He supposed he'd be warmer than Jamie, sleeping rough on the street, at any rate. 'Thanks,' he said. He stood there uncertainly.

Nell was looking at him intently. She seemed to have something on her mind. 'Tom,' she said. 'A wee word of warning.'

'Er . . . yes?'

She stepped closer. 'Don't be too trusting,' she told him. 'People aren't always what they seem.'

'Er . . . ok,' he said.

'I was out on my own when I was your age,' she said. 'Green as grass, I was, and twice as raw. And I had to take some hard knocks before I knew what was what.' She took a deep breath. 'All I'm saying is, not everything in this world is put there for our benefit.' She seemed to decide that she'd said enough. She leaned impulsively forward and pecked him on the cheek, much as Cat had done, though in Nell's case he was aware of the powerful fumes of whisky coming off her. 'Sleep well, young Tom,' she whispered. 'And keep one eye open.'

He was about to ask her how he might manage to do such a thing when she turned and strode out into the night, weaving from side to side as she walked. Tom gazed after her for a moment, wondering exactly what she had meant, but he was too tired to ponder it for long. He turned and surveyed his bed. He could feel exhaustion creeping up on him, so he got down onto his hands and knees and burrowed into the deep straw. Once he was well covered he turned onto his back and gazed up at the roof. He was momentarily surprised to notice that he could somehow still see the stars shining faintly through it. What was he supposed to do if it rained, he wondered. Then he became aware that the straw beneath him was softening, deepening and he was sinking into it as though it had turned to quicksand. Alarm juddered through him and he wanted to scramble upright again, but the strength seemed to have gone from his limbs. He stared upwards at the stars, burning brighter, brighter, until there seemed to be no ceiling above him at all, just the midnight black sky. Then the straw closed around him like a warm, oily wave and he sank into darkness without leaving so much as a ripple . . .

Eight

The softness beneath him shuddered then firmed up until he was aware of hard ground pressing against his shoulder blades. He was still looking at those same stars, except now there was no roof between him and them. He was out in the open air and a cold wind rippled around him, making him shiver. He managed to sit up although his head was woozy and he had to wait a moment to allow a wave of dizziness to pass. Everything came back into focus and he looked around.

He was lying in an alleyway again and for a moment he thought he was right back where he'd started when he'd first arrived in the nineteenth century. Just then he noticed that the rubbish in this alleyway was stored in black plastic bags and a sense of hope sprang up in him. He got unsteadily to his feet and looked along the alley. Yes, he decided, it was the same stretch of cobbled road, leading to a flight of stone steps, but it was the sight of an empty crisp packet, stirring in the breeze, that convinced him he really was back in his own time. Perhaps the unplanned visit had only been a short one.

He hurried along the alleyway, weaving a little at first, but growing steadier as he walked. He reached the narrow road and looked to his left, expecting to see the archway that led into Tanner's Close but it was no longer there. The road was wider and there were houses on only one side of it. He crossed the road and started up the steps, leaning on a metal handrail that he was pretty sure hadn't been there before and he made it to the street above.

The view there was somewhat different than he remembered. The row of houses to his left looked pretty much the same, apart from the odd satellite dish, but the row that had been to his right was gone and the road, covered in smooth black tarmac, was much wider than before and flanked by pavements. As he stood there, deliberating what to do next, lights illuminated him and he saw the familiar shape of a black taxi approaching from the top of the street. He watched as it motored past, the driver intent on the way ahead, two people huddled in the back seat. The red taillights moved on into the night and everything was silent. Tom wondered what time it was. Late, he thought, there didn't seem to be a soul in sight. Well, he knew pretty much where he was, all he needed to do now was to find his way back to Hamish's house in Fairmilehead. Maybe he should try and find a taxi himself?

He looked hopefully around, there wasn't a soul in sight. Perhaps he needed to walk into a busier area. As he stood there, pondering the matter he heard a sound. The slow measured tread of heavy boots clumping on stone. He turned his head, looking this way and that, trying to find the source of the footsteps. They sounded close and yet, he couldn't see anyone . . .

A figure stepped out of the mouth of an alleyway off to his right, a cloaked and hooded figure that stood for a moment, looking at Tom through red, goggled eyes. Tom felt the blood in his veins slow as fear enveloped him in an icy grip. He watched in dread as the figure moved closer, seeming to glide across the intervening space like some phantom. And Tom knew that this time it wasn't just some hapless worker in fancy dress. This time it was real.

The man lifted a gloved hand and pulled the beaked helmet off his head. The thin, wolfish face that grinned at Tom was all too familiar. It was Hamish's face yet at the same time it was also the face of a seventeenth century criminal called William McSweeny, a man who had pursued Tom across the rooftops of Edinburgh and had come uncomfortably close to catching him.

'Hello, Tom,' said McSweeny in that familiar, rasping tone. 'Here you are, at last. I've been looking everywhere for you.'

Tom shook his head. 'No,' he whispered. 'No way. You're . . . you're dead. I *killed* you.'

McSweeny chuckled and shook his head. 'You *thought* you killed me,' he said. 'You *hoped* you did. But you should know, Tom, that I'm no' so easy to get rid of. And I said I'd have my revenge. You remember that, don't you? I said I'd get you for what happened to my mother, no matter where you tried to hide.'

'That wasn't my fault!' protested Tom. 'You were the one pretending to be a plague doctor . . . taking money from people . . .'

'And you're the little rat who told the authorities,' said McSweeny. 'You're the one who pointed me out to them. Did you really think I was going to let you away with that? Is that the kind of man you had me down for?' McSweeny reached a hand to his side and when he lifted it again, a curved blade glittered dangerously in his grasp.

Tom started to back away, his heart hammering in his chest.

'You're . . . you're not real,' he said, desperately. 'You're just a bad dream.'

McSweeny laughed, a deep, rasping chuckle that sent chills crawling down the length of Tom's spine. 'Keep telling yourself that, Tommy, boy,' he whispered. 'You're not real. You're a bad dream. It'll be scant consolation for what's about to happen to you.'

'Wait,' said Tom. 'Please. You've got to–'

He broke off as McSweeny lunged, swinging the blade at Tom's head, and Tom reacted instinctively, dodging to one side. There was nothing dreamlike about that blade. It cut a deadly arc inches in front of Tom's face and the tip of it swung lower and caught the shoulder of his jacket, slicing through the fabric as though it had no more substance than smoke, but thankfully missing the flesh beneath. Tom didn't wait to allow McSweeny another chance. Before the man could raise his arm he sprinted past him, heading along the street.

'Leaving so soon?' cried McSweeny, and when Tom

glanced over his shoulder, it was to see the man's dark figure coming in pursuit, the leather cloak flapping around him like the wings of some huge bat, his long legs covering the intervening space with ease.

Tom looked frantically this way and that, seeking some avenue of escape. The mouth of an alleyway yawned on the far side of the road and he veered instinctively towards it, not knowing what lay in that direction, but absolutely sure that if he stayed on this straight path, McSweeny would catch him and cut him down in minutes. Another steep flight of steps lay ahead of him and he ran up them, three at a time, not even daring to look back. He gained the top, gasping for breath and saw a narrow opening in a wall to his right. He headed for it and his footsteps echoed as he raced into the dark, narrow passageway beyond. A short distance in, the place opened up and in the gloom Tom could see a forest of stone pillars with a narrow aisle between them. He angled left, to hide himself in their midst. He slammed his back up against a pillar and stood there, trying to catch his breath, listening intently.

He heard the footsteps entering the passageway, heavy boots clumping on granite and then McSweeny's voice rang out.

'Oh Tom? Tom? Come on out, why don't you? Come and see what I've got for you. A bright, shiny toy.'

Tom gritted his teeth and tried to still his ragged

breathing. The footsteps slowed. They were close now. McSweeny kept talking, hoping perhaps that Tom would give away his location.

'Remember the wee girl, Tom? What was her name? Morag, wasn't it? She had more courage than you, boy. She came out fighting. She didn't hide like some whipped dog.' A long silence then, 'It's your fault she died, Tom. Do you know that? Your fault. Her blood's on your hands.'

Tom's eyes filled with tears. He wanted to weep but he clamped a hand over his own mouth in an effort to stop himself. The slightest sound would give his position away.

'Tom, I'll make it quick. You'll hardly feel a thing. I promise.'

Now Tom became aware of a shadow lengthening on the ground to his right. He steeled himself. McSweeny was moving past the pillar behind which Tom was hiding. As Tom watched, horrified, the cloaked figure moved into view, his head moving from side to side as he tried to see in the limited light.

'Tom? I know you're in here somewhere. Why don't you–?'

Tom made his move, stepping quickly around the pillar and aiming a wild punch into McSweeny's side. His knuckles connected with something hard, the shock shuddering along the length of his arm and he heard McSweeny gasp in pain, but Tom was already heading back towards the entrance to the passageway. He burst out into the fresh air and stood for a moment, looking frantically around. To his right, a dead end; he'd have to go back the way he came, there was no other choice. He turned and ran towards the stairs, aware even as he did so that McSweeny had burst out of the passageway behind him, his leather cloak flapping in his wake.

'T-o-m-m-m-m!' His voice seemed to reverberate like a clap of thunder.

Tom kept going. The steep stairs lay ahead of him and he had to go down them this time. He was terrified that he would miss his footing and fall, but he didn't dare slow his pace either. He was halfway down the long flight when something heavy thudded against his back and a pair of powerful arms gripped him around the chest. McSweeny's weight swept him off his feet and he was falling, he was twisting around and they were tumbling headlong down the steps in a deadly embrace. Something struck Tom hard between his ribs, slamming the breath out of him and he caught a glimpse of McSweeny's face, inches from his . . . no, not McSweeny, it was Billy, Irish Billy, laughing out loud. And now there was a blanket being pushed into Tom's face, covering his mouth and nose. He was aware of the soft touch of straw beneath him, but he couldn't breath, he couldn't breathe. He struggled, lashed out with his arms, kicked his legs and for a moment he wrenched the blanket away and saw Billy smiling serenely down at him, attempting to push the blanket back into place. Behind him stood Will, holding a lantern, looking calmly down at his friend. Tom tried to speak, but then the blanket was in his face again, cutting off his air and he struggled desperately to free himself. Then he heard a woman's voice shouting, 'What's going on here?' and suddenly he was released. He lay there on the straw, gasping for breath. Billy was looking towards the entrance of the stall and Tom looked too. There was Nell, her hands on her hips, an expression of outrage on her face.

'We . . . we brought a blanket out to the boy,' said Billy, still kneeling in the straw beside Tom. 'I went to put it over him and he went crazy, so he did.'

'That's right,' said Will. 'I think he was dreaming or something.'

'I . . . I was confused,' gasped Tom. 'The blanket . . .'

'I was just trying to put it over you,' said Billy, his face a picture of innocence. 'I thought you might be cold out here. But then you started shouting and kicking like the demons of hell was after you.'

Tom nodded. He shivered and pulled the blanket tighter around himself. 'I had a nightmare,' he said.

Nell stepped into the stall and glared at the two men. 'Get back to your drinking,' she advised them. 'I'll see to the boy.'

Billy got to his feet and grinned at Tom. 'I'd say Nell's taken a shine to ye,' he observed. 'I think you must bring out the mother in her.' He looked at Nell pointedly. 'Business is business,' he said 'Don't forget that.' He walked out of the stall and, after a moment's hesitation, Will followed, grinning his sardonic grin.

'We'll get you another drink in,' he said, as he

passed and he set the lantern back down on the barrel before he left.

'Don't bother,' she shouted after him. 'I'd say we've all had enough for one night.'

She stood for a moment, looking thoughtfully down at Tom. Then she moved closer and settled herself on the straw beside him.

'A nightmare?' she asked.

Tom nodded.

'What's a bright young lad like you done that would give him nightmares?'

'I don't know,' he said. 'Stuff.'

She smiled at him. 'Well, nightmares can't hurt you.'

'Is that right?' He didn't feel convinced. 'What did Billy mean?' he asked. 'About me 'bringing out the mother in you?' Have you got kids?'

Nell sighed. 'I have two children,' she told Tom. 'A boy and a girl. Perhaps I should say, 'had.' I . . . left them with their father in Maddiston when I first met Billy. He was working on the canal there and . . . ah, I let him sweet-talk me into walking away from 'em. I must have been mad or in love. I suppose it amounts to the same thing. The boy would be around your age now. I don't know where my children are or what they're doing. I don't even know if they're still alive. Isn't that terrible?' She looked at Tom and he could see that she was close to crying. Instinctively he reached out and put a hand around her shoulders.

'Why did you leave them?' he asked her.

'Because I listened to Billy and his fancy words,' she said. 'Ah, that man can talk me into just about anything if he puts his mind to it. But there's a limit,' she said. 'There has to be a limit.' She wiped her eyes on her sleeve and smiled at Tom. 'You're a good lad,' she said. 'You'll be all right. You try and get some sleep now.' She lifted his arm away and said, 'I think I'd better find you a needle and thread.'

He looked at her blankly and she indicated the shoulder of his jacket. It was torn wide open, the edges even, as though cut by something very sharp. Fear hit him like a punch to the chest.

'What's the matter?' Nell asked him. 'You've gone white.'

'What you said about nightmares not being able to hurt you,' he gasped. 'I'm not so sure you're right.'

She eased him back down onto the straw and settled the blanket around him. 'Go back to sleep,' she advised. 'I'll see to it that nobody bothers you.' She got up and walked to the exit. 'Do you want me to put that lantern out?' she asked him, stirring the thick straw with one foot. 'It'd be safer.'

He shook his head. 'I'd rather you left it on.'

She shrugged and left the stall. He lay there listening to her footsteps walking away across the yard.

The hours passed slowly and he didn't get very much sleep that night.

Nine

He must have slept eventually, because the next thing he knew, sunlight was in his eyes and he lay there, blinking, remembering where he was and how he had got here. Except that something was different. Now he was looking at the interior of the stable with more experienced eyes, as though he'd actually been here for quite some time. But how could that be? His last real memory was sitting here in the stable, talking to Nell, and the terrible fright he'd felt when she pointed out the tear in his jacket. It seemed to him that this had happened only the previous night and yet . . .

He checked the shoulder of his jacket and saw that it had been neatly sewn up, which confirmed his suspicions. He reached into his pocket and pulled out his mobile phone, to check that the photographs he had taken were still there. But when he pressed the power button, nothing happened. The phone had been on half power last time he'd checked. Now it was completely dead and he had no way of charging it again. He wouldn't know until he got back to his own time if the photographs were still there.

He sighed, pushed the phone back into his pocket and climbed out of the straw. He strolled into the yard where a metal pump stood, exactly where he expected it to be. The weather was colder now, the wind making the skin on his face tingle. He worked the pump's lever a few times to fill an old bucket that stood beneath it and splashed up a little icy water onto his face, noticing as he did so that the sleeves of his jacket looked tattered and grubby, as though he'd been sleeping rough for quite some time. No sooner had he finished washing than he wiped his face on his sleeve and strolled across the yard to the back door of the lodging house. He opened the door and inside, waiting for him, as he somehow knew it would be, was a bucket of food scraps. He lifted the bucket, closed the door and went back across the yard to the stable.

Time's moved on, he told himself. *I've been here for days . . . maybe even weeks. And what I'm doing now is something I do every morning.* He didn't feel unduly alarmed because he'd experienced this kind of thing before, back at Mary King's Close. Instead of returning to his own stall, he opened the door of the adjoining one to reveal several eager-looking pigs that were clearly anticipating his visit. He strolled inside, closing the door behind him, and upended the bucket of food into a battered metal trough. He stood looking down at the pigs' hairy backs as they jostled and grunted after the scraps, and realised that he knew each of them by name. He had to be wary of the big grey one who was called Nessie because she was unpredictable and had been known to take a bite at the legs of careless feeders before now. There was already a sore spot at the back of his right leg where she had caught him a healthy nip and when he looked down he saw that his jeans were torn there and crusted with dried blood.

He hefted the empty bucket and let himself out of the stall, securing the door carefully behind him. He wasn't at all surprised to see Jamie approaching across the yard, a cheery grin on his face, and it was clear that this too, was a daily occurrence.

'G . . . good morning!' said Jamie and as he moved nearer Tom could see that his friend was sporting a nasty-looking black eye.

'What happened to you?' he asked, dropping the bucket and hurrying forward.

'Och. Just some l . . . l . . . lads on the street. They were sh . . . shouting names at me and I answered them b . . . back.'

'Cowards,' muttered Tom. 'Wish I'd been with you. I suppose there was a gang of them?' He tilted Jamie's head back and had a closer look at the bruise. The white of the left eye was an angry red. 'Maybe we should get a doctor to look at this,' he said.

'A doctor? And how w . . . would I pay for that, do you suppose? Och, I'm all right.' Jamie motioned with his head towards the open doors of the barn. 'Come on,' he said, 'Let's have b . . . b . . . breakfast.'

Tom followed him into the empty stall and they settled themselves down. Jamie pushed his bare feet under the deep straw with a sigh of content.

Tom shook his head. 'I don't know why you won't wear shoes,' he said. 'Mary keeps offering to give you an old pair of Fraser's.' Once again Tom had absolutely no idea how he knew this.

Jamie had pulled a cloth bundle from inside his coat and was unwrapping it for inspection. 'I keep telling you, T . . . Tom, that's not the way I r . . . r . . . roll.'

Tom smiled, recognising one of his own favourite expressions. Jamie revealed a unappetising assortment of foodstuffs all jumbled together in his bundle: crusts of old bread, rotten apples, lumps of grey meat, a chunk of watery cheese and some other bits and pieces that weren't so easy to identify. It said something that Tom's stomach didn't recoil at the sight of such an offering. Indeed, when Jamie invited him to 'dig in,' he needed no second bidding. He reached in and pulled out an apple, bit out a worm-eaten chunk and spat it over the wall into the pig's stall, before devouring the rest.

'Where did this lot come from?' he asked, through a mouthful of fruit and Jamie gave a knowing smile.

'Ah, I've got c . . . contacts all over Edinburgh,' he said proudly. 'Everyone knows J . . . Jamie Wilson. When I ask for s . . . scraps, they never say no. But I don't beg,' he added, as though it was important to make a distinction. 'I n . . . never beg. Ask anyone.' He reached into the bundle and pulled out a length of greasy-looking sausage which he broke in half. 'Look at that,' he said, handing half of it to Tom. 'That's q . . . quality, that is!'

Tom took the sausage and had a bite. It tasted slightly off but he wasn't surprised to discover this was now no hardship to him.

'Jamie,' he said. 'How long have I been here?'

Jamie looked at him in surprise. 'D . . . don't you know?' he asked.

Tom shook his head.

Jamie shrugged his slim shoulders. He stuffed the last of the sausage into his mouth and reached into his pocket for the brass snuffbox. He took out the copper spoon and the fingers of his right hand performed their usual rhythmic dance. It didn't take him long.

'Th . . . thirteen days,' he said. 'It's the 22nd of September.'

Tom stared at Jamie. Ok, he thought, that explained why everything seemed so familiar and why there was such a marked change in the weather.

'You still having those d . . . d . . . dreams?' Jamie asked him, as though reading Tom's mind.

Tom looked at him. 'Dreams?' he echoed.

'Aye. About the m . . . man with the crow's head.'

Tom shrugged. 'Now and then,' he said. He wanted to add, 'Except that they're not dreams,' but somehow couldn't bring himself to do it. He swallowed the last piece of sausage and poked around in the bundle for something else.

'What's that?' he asked pointing at a grizzled, round lump nestled in the bundle.

Jamie picked it out and sniffed at it daintily. 'N . . . not sure,' he admitted. 'You want it?'

'Nah, you have it.'

Jamie lifted it to his mouth and took a bite then spat it out again. 'Still n . . . not sure,' he admitted. He tossed it over the wall for the pigs and carried on rooting around in the jumble of scraps. 'You want to g . . . g . . . go and visit the McCallums later?' he asked with a sly smile.

'Oh yeah, great,' said Tom, a little too eagerly. 'I reckon I can get away. Billy and Will never seem to surface before midday, so as long as Margaret doesn't see me, it should be ok. She always finds jobs for me to do. She hates me for some reason.' Jamie handed him a raw carrot and Tom bit the end off it.

'Any s . . . sign of your m . . . mother turning up yet?' asked Jamie.

'Umm. No.' Tom shrugged his shoulders. 'But I never get any warning. It could be just about any . . .'

He broke off as a voice called his name from across the yard. He instantly recognised the shrill tones of Margaret. Tom and Jamie looked at each other and with well-practised ease Jamie grabbed the bundle of food, dived deeper into the straw and spread it over himself. Tom sat there listening as the sound of Margaret's heels came clicking across the yard. Her hulking figure shambled into the stable, her face set in its usual disapproving scowl.

'Still lying abed?' she muttered. 'Have you any idea what hour it is?'

Tom shrugged his shoulders. 'I was tired.'

'Tired of what? You do little enough around this place. Have you fed the pigs yet?

He nodded.

'Well, that's something.' She looked back over her shoulder. 'He's here,' she announced and Will sauntered into the stable. It was unusual for him to be up so early, Tom thought. His nightly drinking sessions usually kept him in bed until after midday.

'Ah, Tom, I'm glad you're here,' Will smiled his insincere smile. 'I have a wee errand for you. A special errand. One that requires a bit of delicacy. It'll be worth tuppence to ye.'

'Oh right, some more knock-off meat, is it? No worries,' Tom assured him. 'When do you need me to do it?'

'Tonight. Late on. It'll be a two-man job. I don't suppose you'd know where to get hold of that halfwit friend of yours?'

'That . . . halfwit?' Tom knew exactly who he was referring to, but wasn't going to give him the satisfaction of confirming it. 'I don't know anyone who . . .'

'I'm talking about Daft Jamie. Would you know where he's to be found?'

Tom tried not to snigger. 'I expect he's around here somewhere,' he said and flinched as he felt Jamie pinch his leg under the straw.

'Something wrong?' asked Margaret, suspiciously.

'I think there might be fleas in this straw,' he said.

Margaret grimaced. 'If there are fleas, they must have come in with you,' she said ungraciously. She turned on her heel and walked away, but Will stayed for a few moments, looking down at Tom. 'Tell Jamie to be here at midnight. There'll be tuppence for him too, but only if he guards his mouth. If I hear tell he's been blabbing about these deliveries, he'll be making no more of 'em. Understood?'

'Understood,' said Tom. He sat looking back at Will, wishing it was Billy he was dealing with. Billy had a way of making any command seem light and informal. Will was just grim and austere and made everything seem underhand. But Billy had already explained what the deliveries were. A few joints of dodgy beef. What was so terrible about that?

'Are we good?' asked Will.

'Yes, Mr Laird.'

Will scowled. 'I told you before, boy. Margaret and me, we're not married. I don't answer to that name. You just call me Will, understood?'

Tom nodded. 'Sorry, Mr La . . . Will.'

Will gave him one last fake smile and turning away, he walked after Margaret. Tom waited until he heard the back door of the lodging house close and then said, 'You can come out now.'

Jamie thrashed himself upward, red in the face. 'That was c . . . c . . . close,' he said. 'T . . . tuppence each!' he added enthusiastically. 'I might buy myself a c . . . cake from the baker's shop.'

Tom scowled. 'I don't like the way he talks about you,' he said.

Jamie looked puzzled. 'The baker?' he muttered.

'No, *Will*! Didn't you hear him? He called you a halfwit.'

'Ach . . . everyone c . . . c . . . calls me that,' said

Jamie, reopening the bundle of food. 'I'm well used to it.'

'Doesn't make it right,' said Tom. 'Can't they see the way you use that snuffbox? You show me any halfwit who can do that. I mean, I can't do sums to save my life. So what does that make me?'

Jamie shook his head. 'The other half?' he suggested.

'And why does Will always go on about not being called Mr Laird?'

'B . . . because it's not his name. That was M . . . M . . . Margaret's old husband.'

'Oh, yeah? What happened to him, then?'

'He d . . . d . . . died,' said Jamie.

'What, a long time ago?'

'A few m . . . months, maybe.'

Tom frowned. 'How did he die?

Jamie shrugged. 'In his s . . . s . . . sleep, they say. Lucky for M . . . M . . . Margaret, she already knew Will. He m . . . moved in a week later.' He rummaged through the bundle of food. 'Come on, let's finish up our b . . . breakfast. Then we'll go and see what the McCallums are up to.' He glanced at Tom slyly. 'Especially C . . . Catriona!'

Tom ignored the dig. They each chose another chunk of something from the bundle, though Tom's appetite was close to being satisfied.

'So how was l . . . last night?' asked Jamie.

'Last night?' Tom frowned.

'Well, when I c . . . came past on the way to my

sleeping place, it s . . . sounded like there was a bit of a p . . . p . . . party going on.'

For an instant an image flickered across Tom's mind. He saw the interior of the lodging house. He saw the fiddle player up at the top of the room, unleashing a merry but cacophonous jig to an appreciative crowd. And he saw Billy and Will and Nell, sitting at their usual table, all of them drinking and drumming their hands on the table-top in time to the music. And in Tom's mind's eye, there was somebody else with them at the table, somebody he didn't know; an old woman with barely any teeth. She was wearing a striped red gown and she had a knitted shawl around her shoulders. She was drinking whisky, and Billy was telling her one of his silly jokes, making her laugh out loud, his arm draped around her skinny shoulders.

The image seemed to shimmer and vanish as abruptly as it had come and Tom could not be sure if this was something he had seen last night or another night or indeed, something he had ever seen. So he could only shrug his shoulders, smile at his friend and choose one last morsel of food for his breakfast, before he and Jamie ventured out onto the cold streets of Tanner's Close, in search of the McCallums.

Ten

They didn't have to look for very long. As they walked along Tanner's Close, they saw Mary and Cat coming towards them, draped in their warm, winter shawls and carrying straw baskets. When she saw Tom, Cat gave a welcoming smile and hurried towards him.

'Tom!' she cried. 'How yer hangin', bro?'

Tom grinned, wondering if he'd been overdoing the lessons on Manchester slang. 'I'm good, thanks. Where are you two off to?'

'We're going to the Grassmarket,' explained Mary. 'We need to pick up a few provisions.'

'Come with us?' suggested Cat. 'Please.'

Tom shrugged. 'I don't mind if I do.'

Cat looked at Jamie. 'And you?' she asked.

Jamie looked decidedly reluctant. 'Oh, C . . . C . . . Cat, you know I hate shopping,' he said. 'It's so b . . . b . . . boring!'

Mary put a hand on his shoulder and smiled at him. 'Why don't you go on up to the house?' she suggested. 'Fraser's there, messing around with those infernal soldiers as usual. I'm sure he'd be glad of the company.'

Jamie grinned, nodded. 'Thanks, Mary. I'll see you tonight,' he told Tom, and sauntered away.

'Oh, what's happening tonight?' Cat asked Tom.

'We're running an errand for Will,' said Tom.

'What kind of an errand?'

'Come along you two,' interrupted Mary. 'All the bargains will be gone if we stand around gassing all day.'

They turned and headed back along the busy street. Mary ran an appraising eye over Tom's dishevelled appearance. 'I hope they're looking after you at Laird's,' she said. 'Your jacket looks like it could do with a good wash.'

'Oh, I'm fine,' he assured her. 'Really.'

'Still no sign of your mother?'

'Er . . . no. Not yet. She'll . . . turn up, though.'

'I hope so, Tom. It must be nearly two weeks now.'

They passed the side street where Laird's was located and walked on until they came to the familiar flight of steps. They climbed to the street above and turned right. The great, grey shape of the castle loomed above them to their left. 'What exactly are we shopping for?' asked Tom.

'Vegetables,' said Cat, wearily. 'And perhaps a wee bit of meat.'

'*Only* if we can find some at the right price,' added Mary.

Tom remembered what Billy had said about the supplier who could get hold of meat at bargain prices. He made a mental note to ask if perhaps the McCallums might be added to the list of 'special' customers. It would be a way of thanking them for all their help. But he decided not to say anything about it until he'd spoken to Billy, just in case such a thing wasn't possible.

'There's a stall on the Grassmarket that sells ribbons and bows,' said Cat, wistfully. 'Perhaps I might treat myself to something there.'

Mary eyed her daughter disparagingly. 'I hardly think you have the money to be wasting on such fripperies,' she said. 'And it's a long time to your next birthday, Catriona.'

Tom slipped a hand into the pocket of his jeans to make sure that his twenty pounds was still where he'd left it, resolving that if he could talk somebody into accepting his English money, *he'd* buy Cat the ribbons she wanted. It seemed the least he could do.

They walked for ten minutes or so and came to the great square of the Grassmarket where row after row of canvas-covered stalls were set out on the busy streets; the vendors shouting their wares to the crowds of people who moved in and out, to stare, to prod and occasionally to spend money. But Tom's attention was, for the moment, captured by a huge sandstone block which stood at one end of the square and into which was mounted a large white cross. Cat noticed him looking at it.

'That's just where the gibbet used to be,' she told him.

He was unfamiliar with the word. 'Gibbet?'

'Where they used to hang people,' she explained. 'You know, bad people. Thieves, murderers, that sort of thing.'

'What? They used to hang them in public?' he cried.

Cat gave him a disbelieving look. 'They still do it in public,' she said. 'Only they moved the gibbet to the Lawnmarket because the crowds got so big.' She shot an annoyed look at her mother. 'Of course, me and Fraser are never allowed to go to the hangings. *Some* people think it's bad for us.'

'I happen to believe it's something that no youngster should ever have to watch,' said Mary. 'For my money, such deeds really ought to be carried out in private. Or better still, done away with altogether.'

Cat laughed. 'That will never happen,' she said. She looked at Tom. 'They must have public hangings in Manchester?' she reasoned.

Tom shook his head. 'No. Now we have something called *The X Factor*,' he told her and left it at that. They moved on into the market and Tom looked around in amazement. It seemed that anything and everything was on sale today. He saw stalls piled high with vegetables; great muddy heaps of potatoes, cabbages and turnips. A little further on was a stall strewn with the bloody carcasses of animals. A man was chopping great hunks of meat into steaks with a cleaver, his striped apron caked with gore while above him hung an array of produce – rabbits with their fur still on, richly feathered pheasants and hanging centrally, the great leering head of a pig, its mouth open, its tongue lolling, a halo of flies buzzing urgently around it.

They walked on some more and came to a large circle of people Peering over the heads in front of him, Tom could see men parading horses before a crowd of appreciative onlookers who stood, drinking tankards of ale and smoking clay pipes, while an auctioneer on a raised wooden stage shouted the bids for each animal. Tom and Cat turned aside and entered another section of the market where crates of live birds were stacked, one on top of the other. Chickens, ducks and geese set up a frantic noise as Tom and his companions moved past and they came to other stalls selling household items – chairs and tables, cups and saucers, brooms and garden tools.

Beggars moved amongst the crowd asking for coins and gangs of feral-looking children roamed around, seeking an opportunity to grab something of value and make a run for it. A street musician wandered by, playing a strange jangling instrument, operated by a lever which he turned with one hand while the fingers of the other framed chords. He was singing something about a 'lad and a lass and a merry frolic all among the hay.' On his shoulder a monkey wearing a pillbox hat and a red military style jacket shrieked and whooped along with him, as though attempting to join in.

Mary approached a vegetable stall and started to poke energetically around amongst the produce, looking for the best offerings. Cat took Tom's hand and pulled him onwards into the crowd.

'Don't go too far!' Mary called after them. 'Tom, mind you keep an eye on Catriona!' Cat waved a hand and flashed Tom a mischievous grin. 'This way,' she urged him. They took a couple of turns between the stalls. Cat clearly knew exactly where she was going. In a matter of moments they were in front of the stall she had mentioned, one festooned with colourful lengths of ribbon, velvet bows and bright shiny buttons. Cat gazed up at the treasures, wide-eyed. 'I love this stall,' she told Tom excitedly. 'I could spend the whole day just standing here, looking.'

A wizened old lady in a frilly white bonnet stood behind the counter, a clay pipe clamped in her mouth. She removed the pipe and smiled a toothless smile at them. 'Something caught your eye, my pretty?' she purred.

'All of it,' said Cat, gleefully.

'What's your favourite?' asked Tom. He slid a hand into his pocket and was about to pull out some money when something caught his eye, a figure in the midst of the crowd on the far side of the stall; a cloaked figure gliding like a ghost through the frantic press of people. Tom felt a chill settle over him as he saw it was a man dressed in a long brown leather cloak. A man with a familiar face. Even as Tom stared in dismay, the figure was turning to look in his direction. William McSweeny's lips curved into a cold, mirthless smile.

Tom reached out instinctively and grabbed Cat's hand. 'Come on,' he said and pulling her along behind him, he headed deeper into the crowd.

'Wh . . . what's the matter?' protested Cat. 'I'd only just started looking!'

Tom glanced over his shoulder to see McSweeny following them, weaving effortlessly in and out of the throng. Tom angled sharp left between two stalls and doubled back on himself.

'Where are we going?' protested Cat.

Tom's mind was racing as he tried to understand what was happening. First McSweeny had been in modern-day Edinburgh and that had been tricky enough. Now he was *here*. How was he managing to cross the centuries as though they had no meaning? And where was Tom supposed to hide to escape him?

Tom headed back the way they had come and saw Mary, still bartering with the man at the vegetable stall, arguing about the merits of a large turnip she was holding. Tom grabbed Cat and virtually thrust her up against her mother. 'Stay here,' he said. 'Don't try and follow me.'

'But Tom, what—?'

He darted away again, hoping against hope that McSweeny hadn't noticed Cat, reminding himself horribly, shockingly, what had happened to Morag in a similar situation to this. She'd tried to defend Tom from McSweeny and had paid for it with her life. He couldn't allow that to happen to Cat. He plunged in where the crowd was thickest, glancing back as he did so. At first he couldn't see McSweeny, and the dread certainty came to him that the man had homed in on Cat and Mary – but then he saw him, still following, craning his head this way and that as he barged his way through the people around him. Tom cursed and tried moving to his left, passing in through a narrow opening between two stalls and pushing his way through the tightly-packed wall of humanity beyond. He emerged from the crush and found himself in the front row of the horse auction. A man was holding a huge shire horse on a halter directly ahead of him and, looking quickly around, Tom could see that the onlookers were packed so tightly there was no avenue of escape. The huge horse barred his path, arching its powerful neck, flaring its nostrils and stamping its heavy feet. The auctioneer gazed sternly across the heads of the assembled crowd and tapped his gavel on a wooden block.

'Who'll bid me ten guineas for this fine creature?' he cried.

'I will!' growled a voice.

'I have ten. Who'll bid me eleven? Come on now, he's a beauty.'

Tom looked frantically over his shoulder to see McSweeny still closing on him, shouldering a path through the crush with no thought for anyone who got in his way. He was grinning confidently now, his teeth bared, and he was reaching under his cloak for something. Tom had a good idea what it was and panic shuddered through him. He looked frantically this way and that, knowing that he only had seconds to come up with a plan of escape.

'Eleven guineas!' he yelled, raising an arm. Every head in the crowd turned to look at him. McSweeny stopped in his tracks, his smile faltering. The auctioneer pointed his gavel at Tom. 'Eleven guineas from the bold young lad down the front there!' he roared. 'Do I hear twelve?'

'Twelve,' said another voice, just to Tom's left; a portly man in a tailcoat and a brocade waistcoat. He was glaring at Tom as though he couldn't believe anybody would have the nerve to challenge him for the horse and Tom edged instinctively closer to him, telling himself that surely McSweeny would do nothing in front of so many witnesses.

'Thirteen guineas,' he yelled and a murmur rose up from the crowd as they sensed some sport. People jostled nearer, wanting to be close to the action and Tom kept edging to his left, closer and closer to the stout man. He glared at Tom, his pudgy cheeks and bulbous nose veined with red.

'Fourteen!' he bellowed, and now Tom could smell the body odour coming off him in waves, but he wasn't going to let that deter him. He got himself shoulder-to-shoulder with the man and glanced quickly around. He couldn't see McSweeny anymore. He became aware that the crowd was silent and realised that everyone was staring at him, waiting to see if he'd bid again.

'Going once,' said the auctioneer. 'Going twice . . .'

'Fifteen guineas,' shouted Tom and there was a gasp of excitement from all around him. Just then Tom became aware of a dark shape moving directly behind him. It felt like the sun going behind a cloud. He sensed rather than saw the knife coming out from under McSweeny's cloak and he reacted instinctively.

He launched himself forward, straight at the Shire horse, aware as he did so that the dark leather-cloaked shape was lunging in pursuit. Tom ducked his head and went under the horse's belly, clearing it by inches. The horse was startled by the sudden movement. It snorted and reared up, then came down hard on whatever was trying to follow Tom. The great hooves pounded the dark shape and flattened it. Tom twisted around with a gasp of triumph, only to see that the horse's feet were trampling nothing more substantial than an empty leather cloak. Tom looked around, licking his dry lips, but there was no longer any sign of McSweeny. He had vanished.

'Going once,' yelled the auctioneer, pointing the gavel at Tom. 'Going twice . . .' Tom stared back at the auctioneer apprehensively, wondering how he was going to explain his way out of this one.

'Sixteen guineas,' bellowed the stout man. 'And not a penny more!'

Tom gazed at him for a moment. For an instant, he even considered putting in another bid, just for the hell of it. But then he asked himself what he would do if he actually *won* the damn thing. Offer them twenty pounds of a currency that didn't even exist yet? So he shrugged his shoulders and turned away, registering the sighs of disappointment from the crowd who had clearly wanted him to win the auction.

Tom made his way back around the circle, keeping his eyes peeled, but there was no sign of McSweeny and something told him that, for the time being at least, he was in the clear. But this latest visitation worried him. If McSweeny could follow him through time, then surely, Tom wasn't going to be safe anywhere. He retraced his steps and eventually found Cat and Mary still hanging around the vegetable stalls. Mary had concluded her business and Cat just looked annoyed.

'What was all that about?' she demanded as Tom wandered sheepishly up to her.

'I . . . er . . . I thought I saw somebody I knew,' said Tom. 'In the crowd.'

'And you didn't want to be seen with me?' Cat looked offended.

'Er . . . no, it wasn't that. I just . . . he's somebody I . . .' He frowned. 'Do you want to go back to the ribbon stall?' he asked.

'No thank you,' she told him, curtly.

Mary eyed them doubtfully. 'What's going on?' she asked them. 'Have you two fallen out?'

'Tom dumped me,' said Cat, indignantly. 'He just pushed me into you and ran away.'

'I noticed that much.' Mary looked at Tom for an explanation. 'Why would you do such a thing?' she asked him. 'It wasn't very gentlemanly.'

'I'm sorry. It's . . . kind of complicated.'

'We're listening,' Cat told him, and he could see that she was determined to know everything.

Tom considered making up another lie, but he was tired of doing that. He sighed as he realised he was going to have to come clean. 'The man in the crowd,' he said. 'The reason I ran away from him. He . . . he's trying to kill me.'

Mary looked horrified. 'Tom, if that's the case, we need to go and see the constables, at once.'

Tom shook his head. 'It's not as straightforward, as you think. The man I saw . . . he's called William McSweeny. And he's from the past.'

'The past?' Cat looked puzzled. 'What do you mean, the past?'

'He's from around two hundred years ago. And, me, I'm . . .'

'Yes?' murmured Mary.

Tom swallowed. 'Well, I'm from the future.'

There was a long silence. Mary and Cat stood there staring at him, their mouths open. He might as well have been talking in Chinese.

Then Cat spoke. 'Tom. You realise how that sounds?'

'I *know* how it sounds,' he assured her. 'I didn't want to have to tell you any of this. But now I guess there's nothing else I can do.' He took a deep breath. 'It all started in Mary King's Close,' he said.

He started talking and he kept on talking until he'd told them everything that had happened to him. And they listened. He could hardly believe it, but they listened to every word he had to say. And when he got to the end of his story, he looked at them and spread his hands and said, 'Well, that's pretty much everything. What do you think?'

Eleven

It was another lively night at Laird's lodging house and the main room was packed with customers. The fiddle player was scraping out one of his awful tunes up on the makeshift stage. Billy, Nell and Will were in their usual places at the big pine table and the drink, as usual, was flowing freely. Tom sat at the table with the others, nursing a tankard of the foul ale that Margaret served, the flavour of which never seemed to improve, no matter how much he sampled it. He kept glancing at the old grandfather clock in one corner of the room as the hour crept steadily towards midnight and he thought about what he had told Cat and Mary, earlier that day at the Grassmarket. Fair play to them, they hadn't told him that he was a raving lunatic, for which he supposed he should be grateful. But neither had they said that they believed him either. In their place, he thought, he'd most likely have some pretty strong doubts himself.

When he'd parted company with them the atmosphere had been strained to say the least – but Cat had given him a polite peck on the cheek and smiled at him, assuring him they they'd see him soon, once they'd had a chance to discuss what he'd told them. He'd walked away wishing that he'd just made up another lie to explain his behaviour at the market.

'A penny for your thoughts?'

Tom looked up and saw Nell smiling at him.

'Oh, just thinking about this job I'm doing later,' he told her. He liked Nell a lot. Despite her fondness for whisky, she was by far the nicest of the crowd here at Laird's and since that first night he'd always had the distinct impression that she was looking out for him in some way. Perhaps Billy had been right when he'd said that Tom 'brought out the mother in her'.

Billy too was extremely likable, always ready with a joke or a funny observation, but in many ways he was a complete mystery. He never seemed to do a day's work and yet, for all that, he was always coming in with a new jacket or hat or a fancy pocket watch. Tom suspected that Nell supported him from whatever kind of work she did. She often disappeared for hours at a time and Tom had occasionally seen her slipping Billy a few coins on the rare occasions when he actually paid for a drink.

Margaret was just Margaret – sour, grumpy, never happy with anything that occurred around the place. If Tom had hoped that she'd warm to him after a while, he was sorely disappointed. She made no pretence of liking him and most of the time was just downright nasty. She delighted in finding more and more menial chores for him to do.

Will was the hardest to fathom of all. He always had that insincere smile on his face, but it never extended to his eyes which were cold and dark and seemed to have the ability to look right through you. Will shared in the profits made at Laird's – though it seemed he spent most of his spare time trying to drink the place into debt, something that Margaret clearly disapproved of. Of course, he and Billy also had their little side line – supplying dodgy meat to various customers around the city, though their main customers always appeared to be the people at Surgeons' Hall. Billy had explained that to Tom.

'Sure, it's all those young medical students. They're ravenous after a hard day's study and ready for some decent grub. That's where we come in. We keep 'em well supplied with our choice cuts and of course, with all them rich parents backing them, they don't mind paying over the odds for it.'

This reminded him that Mary had complained earlier that day about the price of meat at the Grassmarket and he remembered his plan to see if he could get her added to the list of favoured customers.

'Nell,' he said, leaning closer. 'This delivery I'm making later on . . .'

'What about it?' she murmured warily.

'I was wondering if I could get some meat for my friends, the McCallums?'

Nell stole a quick glance at Billy who was busy chatting to Will and then returned her gaze to Tom. She looked suddenly very stern. 'Tom, trust me on this,' she whispered. 'The McCallums wouldn't want what's in those deliveries.'

'Oh, but Mary was saying–'

'Wheesht, Tom! They're honest folk. They wouldn't want to be associated with something that's not one hundred percent legal. This meat that Billy gets, it's – well, let's just say a few corners have been cut. Least said, soonest mended.'

'Er . . . ok.' Tom frowned. 'I'm not sure what that means, exactly.'

'It means the less you know about it, the better.' She looked troubled. 'I didn't really want you involved in the business, but as usual, Billy talked me round. Just do what they tell you and don't ask questions. There's a good lad.' She reached out a hand and patted him on the shoulder.

Tom realised that Will was looking at him now. 'You ready?' he muttered, motioning to the clock which Tom could see was now just a whisker away from midnight. He nodded. Will got up from his chair and motioned for Tom to follow him. As he got up, Nell gave him a worried smile. 'Remember,' she hissed. 'Just do what they tell you.'

He nodded and followed Will up to the top of the room and along the hall to the back door. They stepped out into darkness and Tom was momentarily surprised to see that a thick fog had descended, floating over the yard like a spectre. Will seemed delighted.

'Would you look at that?' he exclaimed. 'That's the luck of the Irish!'

'Why's it lucky?' muttered Tom. 'I can hardly see–'

He broke off as a figure loomed out of the mist. Tom saw to his relief that it was Jamie reporting for duty. Will gave him a brief nod and then beckoned to the boys to follow him to the stable. Just inside the entrance there was a four-wheeled wooden trolley and standing upon it, a plain, wooden tea chest. Tom could see that the lid had been nailed securely shut.

'Well, here it is,' said Will, rubbing his hands together. He reached into the pocket of his waistcoat and pulled out some coins. 'Here we are now, lads. A penny for each of you and the same again when you get back here.' He looked at Jamie. 'You remember where to go?' he asked.

Jamie nodded. 'No p . . . p . . . problem,' he said. 'The S . . . S . . . Surgeons' Hall.'

'Good. You're expected by the night porter. You're to tell him that the contents of this chest are for the eyes of Dr Robert Knox and nobody else. Is that clear?' He looked sternly from one to the other and they both nodded. 'The porter will pay you the sum of ten pounds, which you're to bring back to me.' Tom reached out a hand to touch the top of the chest and Will slapped it away. 'You'll notice the box has been properly sealed to keep the contents fresh and it needs to stay that way. There are very strict rules about the transportation of meat. If the porter notices anything amiss, he'll let me know and the two of you will answer to me. Got it?'

'G . . . got it,' said Jamie.

'Right. Bring it out,' ordered Will.

Tom and Jamie took hold of the trolley and pushed. It took some effort to get the rickety old wheels to roll, but once it was moving they soon had it trundling noisily across the yard towards the loading gate. Will slid back the bolt, opened the gate and stepped out into the road. He looked first in one direction and then in the other. He seemed happy enough and motioned to them to bring the box out.

'Take your time now,' he advised. 'If you see anyone coming, just cool your heels and let 'em go by. They won't bother you.'

'We . . . won't get into trouble over this, will we?' asked Tom.

Will sniggered. 'Don't be daft,' he said. 'Sure, you're only making a delivery, aren't you? You'll be fine.' He clapped his hands together. 'All right, lads, on your way. As soon as you get back, report to me and I'll have your money ready for you.' And with that he strolled back into the yard, closing the gates behind him.

Tom looked at Jamie. 'He's generous,' he observed. 'He gets ten quid and we get tuppence. Does that strike you as fair?'

Jamie shrugged. 'I c . . . can buy a cake for tuppence,' he said.

Tom sighed. 'Which way?' he asked.

'This way,' said Jamie, pointing. They started pushing the cart slowly along the fog-shrouded street. It was an eerie sort of night, the mist so thick they could barely see more than a few feet in front of them.

The streets appeared to be completely deserted which was a blessing because the clattering of the metal-shod wheels seemed to echo in every direction.

'How far is it?' asked Tom.

'Around a half hour's w . . . w . . . walk, with this thing,' said Jamie, nodding at the cart. 'It's up by the Uni . . . v . . . v . . . versity.'

'Let's hope there's no hills.' He strained to get the trolley over a bump in the street. 'This thing is heavy,' he complained.

'Yes. Wh . . . what's in it exactly?'

Tom scowled. 'Didn't I tell you? It's beef. They sell it to the kitchens at the Surgeons' Hall.'

Jamie licked his lips. 'I l . . . love a bit of beef,' he said. 'D . . . d'you think they'd miss a bit if we h . . . helped ourselves.'

'There's no way we . . .'

'Hush!' whispered Jamie. They stopped pushing for a moment and listened intently. The sounds of footsteps came towards them, accompanied by some raucous voices. They stood very still, hugging the shadows as two figures lurched into view; a couple of men, both of them the worse the wear for drink. They had their arms around each other's shoulders and were gabbling nonsense at each other. They weaved unsteadily past Tom and Jamie with barely a glance and the boys were able to continue on their way.

'They w . . . wouldn't know if we took a c . . . couple of handfuls,' muttered Jamie.

'No way! You heard what Will said. You don't want to get on the wrong side of him, do you? Besides, this lid is nailed shut. How do you think we'd open it? With our teeth?'

'G . . . good point,' admitted Jamie.

The journey was pretty uneventful. They saw hardly any people on the way and the few they did see seemed to take no interest in the two ragged boys pushing a trolley. Luckily, there was no sign of the new police officers who sometimes wandered the streets of Edinburgh looking for law breakers. After around half an hour of steady progress Jamie was finally able to point out the gas light that hung over the entrance to the porter's lodge outside the Surgeons' Hall. The boys parked the trolley beside a wall, approached the door of the lodge and tapped gently on the metal knocker. At first there was no answer, so Tom tried pounding it harder. After a few moments the door opened and a man peered blearily out at them, as though he'd just woken up. He was a short, plump fellow in a grubby tailcoat and waistcoat. His head was bald on top, with wisps of long iron-grey hair trailing down at the sides. His cheeks were ruddy and mottled with veins which Tom had already learned was a sign of a hardened drinker. He stared at his visitors for a moment, his mouth open, revealing jagged grey stumps of teeth.

'What time d'you call this?' he muttered. 'They said it would be late, but this is ridiculous. It's nearly one in the morning.' He made a show of pulling a watch out of his pocket and held it out so they could see it, just in case they were in any doubt about the time. Then he tutted and put the watch away. He stood for a moment, his hands in his waistcoat pockets, and stared at the tea chest. 'So, this is it?' he asked them dismally, as though he'd been expecting something grander.

'It's for Doctor Knox,' said Tom, remembering what Will had told him. 'For his eyes only.'

'Yes, yes, I know that! Wait here.' The man stepped out past them and walked along to a double door a little further along. He rapped his knuckles against the wood and, after a short wait, a man opened the door, a tall fellow in a long grey coat. The porter spoke to him quietly for a moment, having to almost stand on tiptoe to whisper in his ear. The tall man's expression didn't change. He turned and shouted over his shoulder and a second man, similarly dressed, appeared beside him. The two men came out and started to manoeuvre the trolley in through the doors.

'We n . . . need the trolley back when you've finished,' Jamie reminded them, but they took no notice. They got the vehicle inside and closed the doors again.

'We're supposed to be paid ten pounds,' said Tom, nervously, worried that the porter might be trying to pull a fast one.

'All in good time,' said the porter. 'All in good time. We have to make sure the meat is of suitable quality. We don't purchase just any old thing, you know.' He looked quickly around as if worried that he might be overheard. 'Actually, you're in luck,' he whispered. 'Old Cyclops is actually here tonight.'

'Old Cyclops?' echoed Tom, mystified.

'Doctor Knox! He's been working late on a complicated bit of surgery. Terrible it was, a woman, knocked down by a brewery wagon. Her legs . . .' The porter screwed up his face. 'But the doctor managed to save one of 'em. She'll be on crutches the rest of her life, but that's a sight better than having no legs at all, wouldn't you say? Oh, he's a great man, Doctor Knox. A genius. They say he'll go down in the history books.'

. Tom frowned. Now that the porter had mentioned it, the name of Knox *did* seem to ring a bell with him, but he couldn't remember exactly where he'd heard it before. A history lesson, perhaps?

The double doors opened and the tall man came out, pulling the empty trolley after him. He parked it and went back inside without a word just as another man stepped out, a distinguished-looking fellow dressed in a long white coat. He too was balding on top of his skull but sported a pair of thick brown sideboards that curved around his cheeks, almost to the edges of his mouth. There was something wrong with one of his eyes, Tom noticed; it appeared smaller and less animated than the other. After a few moments he realised that it was actually a glass eye and he understood why the porter had referred to the doctor, rather uncharitably, as 'Old Cyclops'. Doctor Knox had an almost aristocratic air about him and when he spoke it was in a refined

Edinburgh brogue. 'So,' he said. 'I must confess myself very pleased with the latest consignment.' He reached into his coat and withdrew a leather wallet. 'I believe the agreed fee was ten pounds?' he said.

'Yes, sir, thank you sir.' Tom nodded and held out his hand to take the money. Knox smiled graciously at him.

'Is that an English accent I hear?' he enquired, pressing a paper note into Tom's hand and Tom nodded.

'Manchester, sir.'

Dr Knox smiled. 'I've never visited your city, though I have naturally, in the course of my work, been to London, several times. A most gracious city.' He returned the wallet to his pocket. 'Please convey my best wishes to your employer and tell him I'm always happy to take more of his wares.'

'W . . . we will, sir,' said Jamie, brightly.

Dr Knox studied Jamie's bare feet for a moment. 'Have you no shoes, boy?' he enquired. 'For heaven's sake, you'll catch your death.'

'Oh, I d . . . d . . . don't like shoes, sir,' said Jamie. 'Too uncomfortable.'

Knox raised a quizzical eyebrow at this, but didn't pursue the matter. 'Well, I must get on,' he said. 'I'll bid you good night, gentlemen.' And with that he turned and strode back in through the double doors. They slammed shut behind him.

Jamie walked across to collect the trolley.

'Have you gentlemen got far to go?' asked the porter.

'Tanner's Close,' said Tom.

'Well, mind how you proceed in this fog,' said the porter, strolling back towards the open door of his lodge. 'We wouldn't want you to have an accident, would we? Who'd keep our larders stocked then?' And with that, he went back inside his lodge, closing the door behind him.

'We'll get b . . . b . . . back to Laird's, shall we?' suggested Jamie.

'Ok.' Tom reached out to push the cart, but as he did so the rickety wood seemed to turn to jelly beneath his fingers and he felt a familiar whirling sensation at the back of his skull.

'Oh, no,' he said.

Jamie was looking at him, perturbed. 'T . . . Tom?' he murmured. 'Wh . . . what's wrong?'

Tom opened his mouth to reply, but before he could even say a word he was spinning into darkness and there was no way to stop himself.

Twelve

'Look at those!' said Mum.

Tom opened his eyes. He blinked and stared. The last thing he remembered was trying to push the empty trolley after he and Jamie had made their midnight delivery. Now, suddenly, here he was, back in the museum where everything had started. Mum was pointing to the glass cabinet where the tiny coffins were on display. They were exactly as he remembered them, arranged in a row and lit by tiny spotlights.

'Weird,' he said. He didn't know what else to say. He looked quickly around and everything seemed to be just as it had been when he was last here. Except that this time, it was Mum who was reading the explanatory card beside the coffins.

'Says here there used be seventeen of them,' said Mum 'Some kids found them in 1836 on . . . Arthur's Seat. Hey, we could take a walk up there later if you fancy,' she told him. 'It's a nice day. I'm told it's not so hard if you take your time.'

Tom just stared at her, trying to make some kind of sense of this. He put a hand out to touch the cool glass of the cabinet, wanting to be sure that this was all real and not some dream he was having. But the cabinet felt solid enough. Mum looked at him.

'Are you all right?' she asked him. 'You look . . . strange.'

'I *feel* strange,' he assured her.

Mum frowned and carried on reading. 'Says here the kids didn't know they were worth anything and started throwing them at each other!' She laughed, as though picturing the scene. 'That's why there's only eight coffins left. But this schoolteacher, he realised they were important, so he went back up there and found what was left of them, so . . .'

'Mum,' interrupted Tom. He was having a bad feeling about all of this. 'I think maybe we should leave.'

Mum frowned. 'I thought you were enjoying it,' she said.

'I was. I mean, I am, but . . . you know, it's getting late and . . . I'm hungry.'

'Oh?' Mum glanced at her watch. 'Well, there's a café here, you know. A nice one. I've eaten there before. Couldn't you hang on for a little while, just in case Hamish decides to join us?'

Tom gulped. 'Hamish?' he muttered.

'He was feeling tired this morning so I let him sleep on, but I texted him on the way here, told him where we'd be. If he fancies coming.' She smiled. 'That's ok, isn't it?'

Tom looked at her. *No*, he thought, *that's not a good idea. When he gets here, he'll be drunk and he'll have tickets for the Hibs. And it'll all turn nasty.* But he couldn't tell her that. He'd have to get her away on some pretext. 'Is there . . . is there a loo near here?'

'Yes, dear, just hang on a minute.' She was still intent on reading the card. 'Nobody's sure who put the coffins up there,' she continued. 'There are theories though. Some people thought it might be witches. You know, like voodoo dolls or something? Or it could be they're for sailors that drowned at sea. It says here . . .'

'There you are! I've been looking everywhere for you!'

Tom looked up in dread, expecting to see Hamish's glowering figure prowling between the cabinets towards them. But it was worse than that. Much worse. The man gliding towards them was dressed in a long leather cloak. He had Hamish's features, but the cold mirthless smile belonged to William McSweeny. He strode forward, his gaze fixed intently on Tom.

Mum laughed in disbelief. 'Hamish?' she murmured. 'What's with the fancy dress?'

McSweeny ignored her. He kept his gaze fixed on Tom. 'Face it,' he said, 'You can't escape me. This is your destiny, Tom. You eluded me last time, but you may as well accept your fate.'

'Hamish, what's going on?' Mum started walking towards him, putting herself front of Tom. 'Is this some kind of a jo −?'

McSweeny didn't slow his pace. He raised one arm and struck her hard across the face with the back of his gauntlet-covered hand. She reeled aside with a cry of shock and collided with a glass cabinet, overturning it. It struck the ground and exploded into smithereens, spilling its precious contents onto the floor. Mum sprawled in the midst of the wreckage, seemingly knocked cold.

'Mum!' Tom took a step towards her, but froze as McSweeny reached into his cloak and his hand emerged, wielding a knife. He scythed a deadly arc inches in front of Tom's face and kept right on coming.

'Come on, Tom,' he hissed. 'Take your punishment like a good boy.'

Tom began to back away along the aisle, glass cabinets to either side of him. He glanced helplessly around, searching for some kind of protection and he spotted an exhibit on the wall to his left, a huge double-handed broadsword in a jewelled scabbard. He grabbed at it instinctively, thinking it would just come away, but realised in an instant that it was fixed securely in place. McSweeny laughed as Tom tugged ineffectually at the sword.

'Pathetic,' he said and raised his arm to strike.

Tom put everything he had into one last, desperate pull, straining with all his might. The fixings tore out of the wall in a shower of grit and plaster and Tom swung around to face McSweeny, holding the sword horizontally in front of him just as McSweeny's arm descended. The man's wrist struck hard against the jewelled scabbard and he cursed as the knife slipped from his grasp and went skittering across the floor. Tom didn't waste any time. He took the sword by the handle and pulled it loose from its scabbard, then tossed the sheath away. He gripped the weapon with both hands and swung the heavy blade from side to side as he began to advance on McSweeny, who had suddenly lost his confident smile.

'Come on then,' hissed Tom through clenched teeth. 'Come on, if you think you're hard enough.'

McSweeny laughed. 'You haven't got the guts to use that blade,' he said, but now it was he who was backing away, pieces of glass from the shattered cabinet crunching under his heavy, metal-shod boots. He glanced down at Tom's mum, as though debating taking her hostage, but Tom hurried forward to head him off.

'Don't even think about touching her,' he snapped and McSweeny continued to back away. Tom lifted the heavy sword above his head. 'I'm sick of being chased,' he growled. 'Now let's see how you like it.' And with that, he gave a yell and ran at McSweeny, the sword held ready to strike. McSweeny's nerve failed him. He turned and fled, back the way he had come, heading for the swing doors at the top of the room, his cloak flapping behind him. He reached the door, threw it open and ran into the corridor beyond. Tom raced after him, determined not to let him escape, but as he burst through the doorway, he had to rein himself in, when he saw an elderly man and a young girl standing a short distance away, staring at him in absolute terror. The man's arm went around the girl and he pulled out a wallet. 'Take whatever you want!' he gasped. Tom swerved past the couple and saw that McSweeny was heading down the staircase, running now for all he was worth.

'Sorry!' yelled Tom as he followed McSweeny, descending the staircase as fast as he dared. McSweeny made it to the next floor, which was crowded with tourists. There was some incredulous laughter as he came pounding down the stairs, but they turned to yells of terror as they saw a boy armed with a broadsword, running in hot pursuit and yelling like a maniac. People scattered in all directions and a security man started shouting something into a walkie-talkie. McSweeny threw open the door of the next gallery and ran inside. Tom was intent on nothing more now than getting his man and he followed. He saw McSweeny up ahead of him, running through the crowded gallery, barging people aside in his eagerness to escape.

'What's the matter?' bellowed Tom, his voice echoing around the gallery, as all heads turned to look at him. 'Not so brave now, are you?'

McSweeny was heading towards the central display, the full skeleton of a Tyrannosaurus Rex, which towered above the customers, its great jaws open. As McSweeny tried to veer around the display, his feet slipped on the tiled floor and he went down in a sprawl. Tom gave a cry of triumph and quickly closed the gap between them. He stopped a short distance away and approached McSweeny slowly, the sword held above his head. People looked on in mute horror. McSweeny scrambled around onto his backside, breathing heavily. He began to edge away, pushing himself with his feet, his gloved hands held up in a pleading gesture. He kept moving until he stopped with a thud against the plinth on which the dinosaur skeleton stood.

'Wait, Tom,' he said. 'Let's . . . let's talk about this!'

'There's nothing to say,' said Tom, grimly. 'Except goodbye.' And with that, he brought the sword down hard, with every intention of splitting the man's head open. But at the last moment, McSweeny swung sideways and it became clear that Tom had underestimated how long the sword was. The end of the blade struck the plinth, hacking clean through one of the dinosaur's feet with a loud clang. For an instant, there was nothing but a deep, shocked silence. Then a creaking noise from above caused Tom to look up at the great bony beast's head. It looked, momentarily, as though it had come to life. It was moving, tilting, twisting, the jaws hinging further open, the jagged teeth glittering in the light. And then, with shocking suddenness, the whole gleaming construction came down onto Tom in an avalanche of bone and he was lost in a blizzard of tumbling white shards, raining down on him like a biblical hailstorm. In the midst of the chaos, a gauntlet-covered hand reached up and grabbed him by the throat . . .

Thirteen

Tom gasped, clutching at his throat, still feeling the power of those gloved fingers squeezing his windpipe. It took him several moments to realise where he was, standing in the yard at Laird's Lodging House, gazing down into a bucket of water that he must have filled from the pump. He had to throw out a hand to the pump to steady himself while he waited for his heart to settle back to a more regular rhythm. There was a thick sheen of sweat on his face, despite the chill of early morning. He leaned over and splashed some icy water onto his face in an attempt to bring himself back to reality. Then he realised that somebody was behind him. He turned and saw a young woman standing a short distance away from him, a woman he had never seen before. She was looking at Tom, uncertainly, as though unsure of what to say.

'Can I . . . help you?' he croaked.

The woman came a little nearer. She was a rough-looking sort, Tom decided, her once-pretty green dress tattered and stained, her hair hanging around her face in disarray. Like Nell, her features were whitened with powder and her eyes outlined in black. She held a red velvet purse in her hands.

'Do you work here?' she asked him.

'Umm . . . yeah. Sort of.' Tom shook the last shreds

of dizziness out of his head, but he couldn't seem to rid himself of that final image. McSweeny's hand closing around his throat in the midst of a blizzard of falling bone. He swallowed hard. 'Are you . . . looking for a place to stay?' he asked. 'I think we might have a room.'

'No. I'm looking for my mother,' said the woman.

'Your . . . mother?' Tom was puzzled. 'I'm sorry, I don't . . .'

'Her name's Mary. Mary Haldane. Do you know her?'

Tom shook his head. 'No, sorry, I've never heard that name.'

The woman shook her head. 'It's just that I'm very worried about her. She didn't come home the night before last and that's not like her. I waited all day yesterday and all last night, too and . . . well, I'm worried. I'm Peggy, by the way. Peggy Haldane.'

'I'm Tom.' He lifted an arm and wiped his wet face on his sleeve. 'But . . . what makes you think I'd know where she is?'

Peggy frowned. 'I did some asking around. I spoke to a woman who told me she thought she saw my mother, two nights ago, with that feller they call Irish Billy. Do you know him?'

'Billy? Yeah, I know him. He's my friend.'

'This lady is pretty sure it was him. She said they looked like they was friends and all. He had an arm around her shoulders and they was walking up the close towards this place, looking like maybe they was after a drink or something. Could she have come here?'

'Well, we get a lot of people in at night,' admitted Tom. 'Most of them like a drink. But I don't know if your mother came here. What does she look like?'

'Och, just an old lady with white hair. Hardly any teeth.'

That made Tom take notice. It came to him then, the image he'd seen in his head that time, an image of Billy sitting at their usual table in Laird's with an old lady beside him. Billy was joking with her and had an arm around her shoulders. He looked at Peggy, not wanting to alarm her. There was only one question to ask next. 'Did your mother . . . I mean, was she wearing a red striped dress?'

'She was!' said Peggy, excitedly. 'You *have* seen her!'

'Umm . . . well, I kind of *think* I might have,' admitted Tom.

Peggy came a step closer. 'What do you mean?' she demanded. 'You kind of think? Either you've seen her or you haven't. Which is it?'

'What's going on here?' demanded a voice and they both turned to see that Margaret standing on the step by the back door, her hands on her ample hips. She studied Peggy with her beady black eyes and didn't seem to like what she saw. 'Who are you?'

'This is Peggy,' said Tom. 'She's . . .'

'Wheesht! I'm sure the lady is quite able to speak

for herself,' said Margaret coldly. She kept her gaze fixed on Peggy. 'Well?' she demanded.

'I'm looking for my mother. Mary Haldane. She went missing two nights ago and this boy here was telling me that he thinks she might have come here with that Irish Billy.'

There was a silence while Margaret absorbed this information. She looked at Tom for a moment and her eyes flared with some kind of inner anger. But that settled after a moment. She returned her gaze to Peggy and her features quickly rearranged themselves into an expression of relief. She came down off the step and hurried across the yard. 'So *you're* Peggy!' she gasped. 'Thank the Lord. Mary has been asking for you and we didn't have the first idea where we might find you.'

Peggy lifted one hand to clutch at her throat. 'Asking for me?' she whispered. 'What do you mean? Is something . . . wrong with her?'

Margaret slipped a meaty arm around Peggy's shoulders. 'Now, you're not to worry, my dear,' she said. 'Mary was here the other night, and she . . . well, she took a bit of a bad turn, so she did. Came over all dizzy. At first we thought it was the whisky, but then I realised it was more than that. I didn't know what to do for the best, so we put her to bed. She's very weak, poor thing and a little delirious. But all she kept asking me, every time I went in to check on her, was that she wanted to see her Peggy. We didn't know where to look and Mary, poor lamb, was quite incapable of telling us. But now, thank God, here you are.' She started to pull the woman towards the door. 'Mary's sleeping just now, but I think a stiff brandy would be good for you, while you're waiting for her to wake up.'

'How bad is she?' whimpered Peggy. Tom could see that she was close to tears now. 'She's . . . she's not going to . . . ?'

'Oh, now don't you fret, my dear. She's as strong as an ox. I'm sure a couple of day's rest will see her straight.'

'But . . . I don't know how we'll pay for the room,' protested Peggy.

'Oh, don't you worry about that! We wouldn't dream of asking you for one penny. That would hardly be the Christian thing to do.' Margaret turned her head and looked at Tom. 'Boy, I want you to run straight to Rymer's shop. You'll find Billy having his breakfast there. Tell him I need him, right away.'

'Yes, Margaret.'

'Tell him Mary's daughter's here and she's concerned for her mother. Oh, and as soon as you've done that, I want you to go on to the baker's shop in the Quartermile and ask him for a loaf of rye bread. Tell him to put it on our account.'

Margaret led Peggy towards the back door and Tom got himself moving. He let himself out of the yard and started walking briskly along the close. He'd gone some distance before it occurred to him that something here didn't quite make sense. If Mary Haldane was ill and had been lying in a bed at Laird's for a couple of nights, how come nobody had ever mentioned it to him? Margaret didn't tell him everything, of course, but surely he'd have overheard her talking about it to Billy or Will? He shook his head, trying to push the idea away, but for all that, he still felt unsettled.

After ten minutes, he came to Rymer's and went inside. Sure enough, Billy was sitting at a table in the low-roofed, rough-timbered bar, eating ham and eggs and talking loudly to the portly barman and a couple of regulars, who, despite the early hour, were already getting stuck into drams of whisky. When Billy saw Tom, he stopped talking and studied the boy.

'What are you doing here?'

'Margaret sent me. She says she needs you at the house, straight away.'

Billy sneered. 'She'll have to wait till I've finished my breakfast,' he said. 'I'm not hurrying myself on her account.'

'It's just that a woman called Peggy Haldane came looking for her mother. Margaret took her inside to see her.'

Billy's eyes narrowed. He seemed to be thinking about something. He got up from the table. 'You know what?' he said. 'I'm not really that hungry.' He gestured at the barely-touched meal. 'Tell you what, Tom, why don't you finish this for me? I dare say you could use something decent inside you. Better than the muck that Jamie brings you every morning.'

Tom looked at the meal and his stomach rumbled. It looked a hundred times better than the bits and pieces he usually settled for. 'Umm . . . it's just that Margaret wanted me to go to the bakers on the Quartermile,' he said. 'So . . .'

'Ah, there's no hurry for that!' Billy assured him. He pushed Tom down into the vacant seat. 'You take your time now,' he said. 'Sure, the baker's doesn't even open for another hour.' He gestured to the bar. 'Bring the lad some more bread and butter and a sup of tea to have with this,' he told the barman. 'Put it on my account.' And with that, he winked at Tom and went out of the bar, into the street.

Tom picked up Billy's knife and fork and went at the meal with a vengeance, cramming his mouth full of food and using the slabs of bread and butter to mop up the meat juices and egg yolk. After the slim pickings he been forced to eat lately, this tasted like heaven on a plate.

It was only when his hunger had been properly sated that he thought once again about Mary Haldane. If she really was ill somewhere in the lodging house, surely Nell would have said something? The two of them spoke often and chatted about most things that went on at Laird's. He sighed. He took a last slurp of tea, got up from the table and with a nod to the barman went out onto the high street. Again, something struck him as odd. Margaret had never sent him to the baker's before. And why would she choose one that was so far from home and moreover, one that wasn't even open for business?

He shook his head. He was too wary of Margaret to question her orders, so he walked all the way up to the Quartermile, waited twenty minutes for the shop to open, got the loaf of bread and retraced his steps back to Laird's. He went in at the back door and found Billy, sitting at his usual table, eating a bowl of watery porridge. It looked like a poor substitute for the meal he had abandoned back at Rymer's. Tom set the loaf down on the table top.

'Here's the bread Margaret wanted,' he said.

'Good timing,' observed Billy, grinning. 'I'll have a slice straight after I've finished this.'

'Thought you weren't hungry?' said Tom.

'I got my appetite back,' said Billy, with a shrug.

'For Margaret's porridge?' asked Tom, incredulously.

'Ah, you get a taste for it, it's not so bad.'

'How's Mary?'

'Ah, the strangest thing,' said Billy. 'As soon as she set eyes on her daughter, she made a miraculous recovery. Sprang up out of that bed like a twelve-year-old, so she did. The two of them set off for home not ten minutes ago. You just missed 'em. But Peggy said to thank you for all your help.' Billy spooned porridge into his mouth and gulped it down. 'By the way, your friend Jamie is waiting for you out in the stable.'

'Oh, right. Thanks.' Tom turned and headed for the door. 'He seemed worried about you,' added Billy mysteriously. 'Said something about you disappearing the other night?'

'Oh . . . er, yeah . . . I . . . I'd better go.'

Tom let himself out and crossed the yard to the stable. As he neared the entrance, Jamie came out, looking concerned. 'T . . . Tom!' he said. 'You're back. I was g . . . getting really worried. And when you weren't here this morning . . .'

'I had to do an errand for Margaret,' Tom assured him. 'I'm fine.'

'B . . . but what happened to you last n . . . night? Where did you go?'

Tom stared at Jamie, remembering what had happened back at the Surgeons' Hall, how his friend must have seen him disappear, right in front of his eyes.

'Jamie, it's going to sound really weird. But . . . I'll try and explain while we eat.' He followed Jamie into the stable and the boy gestured at something that was sitting on top of the barrel, just inside the doorway. A big round cream cake.

'L . . . l . . . look what I got us!' cried Jamie delightedly. He was so excited, he was almost dancing a jig.

Tom stared. For once in his life he had a full stomach but there was always room for cake. 'How much did that cost?' he protested.

'Tuppence,' said Jamie, leading him inside. 'It's a good job you're b . . . back, or I would have had to eat it all by m . . . myself.' He grinned, showing his rotten teeth. 'D . . . don't worry, by the way. I've still got your tuppence. W . . . Will said to pass it on to you.'

'You shouldn't go spending all your money like that,' Tom chided him. 'But I'm glad you did. I'll give you half the money.'

'Oh it d . . . d . . . doesn't matter,' Jamie told him. 'We'll be paid the s . . . same again tonight. Just try not to d . . . d . . . disappear on me this time!' He pointed and Tom turned his head to look.

The four-wheeled trolley was parked just inside the door. On it stood another tea chest, the lid nailed shut.

Fourteen

I'm going to be stuck here forever, thought Tom bleakly. He lay in the stall, gazing around at the grim, smelly stable that was now his domain. Since making the second trip up to Surgeons' Hall with Jamie – twelve pounds for the contents of the tea chest that time and no sign of Doctor Knox – the days had slipped steadily past. Now here it was, mid October, the weather getting bitterly cold and there was no sign that he was ever going to find his way back to his own time.

He was starting to feel depressed. For one thing, he looked and smelled like a tramp. He'd had no opportunity to change any of his clothes since he'd arrived here or even to have a proper wash, apart from the habitual splash of freezing water from the pump in the yard. His jacket was virtually falling off him, his trousers gone at the knees and his precious iManc T-shirt looked like something the cat had dragged in. Any attempts to ask Margaret if he might have a bath somewhere in the lodging house had been met with terse refusals. Did he have any idea how much it cost to heat up a tin tub of water? Such things had to be reserved for paying guests!

The other problem was that there wasn't much variety in his life. Every morning, he breakfasted with Jamie and whenever they could get away, the two of them visited the McCallums (seeing Cat was the one bright spot in an otherwise gloomy landscape). But lately, during the day, Margaret had taken to giving Tom every menial job she could think of – washing pots and pans, cleaning floors, running errands all over the city, so finding the opportunity to get away was difficult to say the least. In the evenings he was expected to hang around Will's drinking den, collecting tankards and watching as a motley collection of wastrels drank themselves insensible. Occasionally there was a fight to break up the monotony. Usually it was a couple of customers who'd fallen out with each other, but on one memorable occasion it had actually been Margaret and Nell who'd come to blows. Tom had been aware from the start that the two women had a low regard for each other, but this had been a screaming, cursing, hair-pulling catfight with the two women insisting that the other had been giving them 'the evil eye.'

Afterwards, Nell had been all for leaving the lodging house and finding accommodation elsewhere and indeed, she and Billy had taken themselves off for a few days to stay with Billy's brother in Gibb's Close. But after a short absence they came back rather sheepishly and moved into their old room. Billy said that he'd been missing the booze and Nell, she simply had to swallow her pride and make the best of it.

The only encouraging thing was that since his weird experience in the National Museum Tom had seen nothing more of McSweeny and he was beginning to think that his bad dreams – if indeed, that's what they were – had finally worked themselves out of his system. But, given his current situation, it was hard to see the good side of anything.

He sensed movement out in the yard and right on cue Jamie appeared at the entrance of the stall, grinning away and proffering his usual bundle of scraps. No fancy cake this morning. His bare feet were blue with the cold but he seemed oblivious to the fact.

'G . . . g . . . good morning!' he said cheerily. 'How's T . . . Tom today?'

'I'm all right,' grunted Tom although his tone made it quite clear that he was really quite the opposite.

'What's the m . . . matter?' asked Jamie, coming forward and settling himself into his usual spot. 'Still worried about g . . . getting back to your own t . . . time?'

After what had happened on that first visit to Surgeons' Hall, he'd had no option but to tell Jamie all about it. Jamie had actually seen him disappear, for goodness sake, and had been left to push the wooden cart back to Laird's all by himself. When he'd got back he'd made up some excuse to explain Tom's absence because he couldn't quite believe what he'd seen with his own eyes, and there was no way he was going to tell Billy and Will what had really happened. So the following morning, while they sat devouring a whole cream cake, Tom had been obliged to tell Jamie everything, from his first trip to Mary King's Close to his arrival in Tanner's Close. Jamie had listened enthralled and typically of him, had accepted the story without hesitation. This was more than could be said for the McCallums, who, since first being informed of Tom's strange situation, had never mentioned the matter again.

Mind you, *they* hadn't seen Tom disappear right in front of their eyes.

'It's not about that,' said Tom. 'I know I'll get back sooner or later. At least, I'm pretty sure I will. It's just–'

'Wh . . . what?' persisted Jamie. 'You l . . . look sad.'

Tom sighed. 'I'm . . . fed up with everything,' he complained. 'I mean, look at me!' He spread his arms open so that Jamie could get a better view of his general shabbiness. 'I look a complete dosser. At home I was a sharp dresser. I used to have a shower every morning.'

'What's a sh . . . sh . . .?'

'It's like a bath, only you stand up?'

Jamie looked horrified. 'A bath every morning? Oh, T . . . Tom, that's not healthy!'

'Oh, but it is. *This* isn't healthy, sitting around in smelly clothes, eating other people's leftovers.' He glanced at Jamie who was just unwrapping his bundle of scraps. 'No offence,' he said. 'But . . . where's the cornflakes? The fresh milk? The *toast*? I'd kill for some peanut butter and jam!'

'I could p . . . probably get some jam,' said Jamie. 'But what's p . . . pea . . .?'

'Never mind,' said Tom, crossly.

139

'I've g . . . got some nice stuff this morning. L . . . look!' Jamie waved his hands over the mess of scraps as though he was offering Tom a luxurious 'all he could eat' buffet. He pointed. 'See that there? That's a genuine p . . . p . . . pig's trotter.'

'Oh, lush! You can have that, with my blessing,' Tom assured him. 'I'm really not hungry.'

'Och, c . . . come on, you have to have s . . . something to keep b . . . b . . . body and soul together. Hey, maybe Billy will have another errand for us soon and we can b . . . buy another cream cake!' Jamie leaned back on one arm and his hand sank into the straw at the corner of the stall. His expression changed. 'What's this?' he asked, puzzled. He withdrew his hand and he was clutching a red velvet purse. 'This y . . . yours?' he asked.

'Course not,' muttered Tom. 'That's a woman's bag.' But the sight of the purse stirred something within him. He'd seen it somewhere before, recently, he thought. He could picture it clutched in a woman's hands . . .

Jamie had opened the purse to look inside it. 'It's empty,' he said, sounding quite disappointed. He made to put it into his pocket. 'But maybe I can get a p . . . penny for it on the m . . . market.'

'Hold on, you can't just take it. Somebody might be looking for that.' Tom reached out and grabbed the purse from Jamie's hands. 'I wonder how it got here?' he said, staring at it.

'I suppose somebody must have d . . . d . . . dropped it,' suggested Jamie.

'But nobody ever comes here. Except . . .' Then Tom remembered. 'Wait!' he said. 'The woman who called, she had a red purse! I'm sure she did.'

'What w . . . woman?' asked Jamie, selecting a handful of something unspeakable from his bundle. 'Nell?'

'No. The woman who came here looking for her mother. Haldane, I think her name was. Yes . . . Peggy Haldane.'

Jamie frowned. 'That's f . . . funny.'

'What is?'

'S . . . somebody was only asking me about them the other day. P . . . Peggy. Her mother is called M . . . Mary, right?'

'Yeah, that's them. Who was asking?'

'Oh, j . . . just a woman I know. She s . . . stopped me on the street. Asked me if I'd seen either of 'em. Said p . . . people were worried about them, because they've g . . . g . . . gone missing.'

'Missing?' Tom tried to recall exactly what had happened when Peggy had paid him that unexpected visit. 'Well, what happened was, the mum was over in the lodging house having a drink and she was taken ill. So Margaret let her have a room. And then Peggy turned up, dead worried and everything, and Margaret was really nice to her . . .' Tom stopped talking. Jamie was giving him a disbelieving look.

'M . . . M . . . Margaret was *nice* to somebody?' he cried. 'Are you sure?'

Tom smiled. 'Er . . . yeah. Now you mention it, it does sound kind of odd, doesn't it? But seriously, she was dead welcoming. Took her over to the house for a drink of brandy. She sent me off to get Billy and then I had to do this errand for her. Took ages. By the time I got back, the two women had . . . well, they'd gone.'

'When *was* this?' asked Jamie, chewing a mouthful of gristle.

'Oh, a while back. It must have been . . . yeah, it was the same day we took that tea chest over to the Surgeons' Hall . . .'

'The t . . . time you disappeared?'

'No, the very next night. You remember . . . you spent all the money on cake. You got a great big . . .'

He stopped talking as he saw that Jamie was staring past him towards the entrance of the stall. Tom lifted his head to see Margaret standing there, regarding the two of them in silence. Tom had no idea how long she'd been there or how much she'd heard.

'Margaret,' he said. "We were just . . .'

'What have you got there?' she asked, pointing.

'Oh, er . . . this?' Tom lifted the purse. 'Jamie found it in the straw,' he said. 'I think it belongs to Peggy Hal . . .'

'It's mine,' said Margaret, stepping forward into the stall. 'Been looking for it everywhere, I have. A present from Will, for my last birthday.'

'Oh, but I thought it looked . . .'

Before he could protest Margaret reached down

a meaty hand and pulled the purse from his grasp. 'I hope you two haven't spoiled it with your greasy hands,' she said. 'This is my favourite, this is.' She looked accusingly at Jamie. 'You sure you found it? You haven't been snooping around in the house and helping yourself to a few things?'

'No, Margaret, I was with him when he found it,' protested Tom. 'It was hidden in the straw, honest. Jamie's no thief.'

'Humph.' Margaret looked down with evident disgust at the bundle of scraps, lying on the straw. 'What's all this?' she cried.

'It's . . . breakfast,' said Tom, dismally.

'Good Lord! It's a wonder you two don't make yourselves ill, eating a mess like that,' she observed.

Jamie stared up at her defiantly. 'T . . . Tom has to eat *something*,' he said. 'And y . . . you don't bother f . . . feeding him, do you?'

Margaret stared down at him, her eyes glittering with venom. 'And who are you to question me?' she sneered. 'A street beggar. A beggar and a halfwit.'

'I'm n . . . no beggar,' protested Jamie. 'Ask anyone.'

'And he's no halfwit either,' added Tom, for good measure. 'He's one of the brainiest people I know.'

Margaret laughed. 'He doesn't even have my permission to be here,' she said. 'Jumped-up little puppy thinks he can come and go as he pleases.' She leaned closer and looked Jamie in the eye. 'Billy might have a soft spot for you . . . and that painted tart he calls his wife . . . but you don't impress me, Jamie Wilson, not one wee bit. A word from me and you won't see your English friend, here, ever again.'

Jamie seemed to be close to losing his temper. 'I'll s . . . see whoever I like,' he snarled. 'You c . . . can't tell me what to do!'

'I can tell you what I like when you're trespassing on my property!'

'Margaret, he was just visiting me,' pleaded Tom. 'He . . . he wasn't doing any harm.'

'I'll be the judge of that.'

Jamie glowered at her. 'You think I want to be here? I'm only looking after Tom because you're doing a t . . . t . . . terrible job. And d . . . don't you think it's funny that P . . . Peggy Haldane's purse is here, when everybody on the street knows that she's gone m . . . m . . . missing?'

'It's *not* her purse!' retorted Margaret. 'It's mine. And I'll thank you to mind your own business.'

'It does *look* like Peggy's purse,' said Tom.

Margaret rounded on him. 'What do you know about it?' she screamed. 'I won't be questioned by two beggars! I'm a respectable landlady with a business of my own.' With that she launched a kick at Jamie's bundle and scattered its contents all over the stall. 'Clear this mess out and take yourself off with it. I'll not have you here again, you're not welcome, Jamie Wilson. Tom, I need you in the kitchen, there's work to be done.'

'But . . .'

144

Margaret grabbed a length of rope from a hook on the wall and took a threatening step towards Tom. 'Stay out of it,' she said, 'unless you want me to pepper your britches for you.' She turned back and glared at Jamie. 'I'm waiting,' she snarled. 'Or do you want me to help you on your way, *Master* Jamie?'

Jamie stared back at her for a moment, but then his nerve seemed to fail him. He got reluctantly to his feet, grabbed what was left of his bundle and slunk towards the doors. 'I'll see you l . . . later,' he muttered to Tom as he went by. 'When the w . . . witch is in her lair.'

Margaret spat out an oath and lunged towards Jamie, and he took to his heels and ran across the yard, out of sight. Margaret turned round in the doorway. Tom had never seen her so angry. Her eyes were bulging and her face was bright red.

'I don't know why you're so angry with him,' said Tom. 'He only . . .'

'I will *not* be questioned in my own home, especially not by the likes of him,' said Margaret. 'And you'd do well to watch your mouth, also. You're only here because of Billy's silver tongue. If I had my way, you'd never have set foot in this place. Now, there's a big stack of dirty dishes in the kitchen waiting for your attention. And when you've finished them, there are fires to be laid and floors to be swept and bed pans to be emptied. So get to it.'

Tom trudged dejectedly out of the stable and across the yard, wondering why he didn't just run away. Maybe sleeping rough on the streets with Jamie would be preferable to this. It wasn't as if he was being paid for his trouble.

He went in at the back door and along the hall. Billy was sitting at his usual table, reading a newspaper and drinking tea. He looked up as Tom entered and grinned his amiable grin. 'Here's the boyo,' he observed. 'What's up with you? You look like you found a shilling and lost two!'

Tom shrugged. 'I've just had a tongue-lashing from Margaret,' he said.

'What else is new?' Billy laughed softly. 'What was it this time?'

'Jamie found a purse in the stable. I think it was left here by Peggy Haldane, but Margaret says it's hers.'

'Peggy Haldane? Oh, that bit of baggage that came asking after her mother? Ah, don't be worrying yourself over that one. Her and the old woman was only tryin' to get money out of Margaret.'

Tom frowned. He'd thought Peggy seemed all right.

'How do you mean?'

'Sure, they've pulled that trick all over Edinburgh. The old one pretends to get sick and then the daughter comes a lookin' for her. Then they try and blame the sickness on the food or the drink you served and they demand money or they'll tell everyone not to bring their custom around.' He gave a dismissive snort. 'We saw through that quick enough. Sent them on their way, so we did.'

'Jamie reckons people are saying the two of them have gone missing.'

'Is that a fact? Trying their luck in another town, I expect.'

Just then the door opened and Margaret came into the room. She still had the rope in her hand. She glared at Tom. 'I thought I told you to get to work,' she snapped.

'Yeah, yeah, I'm on my way,' he assured her and headed out of the room and along the corridor to the kitchen. Billy tipped him a sly wink as he went. At the top of the corridor Tom glanced back and saw that Margaret was now sitting at the table opposite Billy. The two of them were talking quietly, their heads bowed, as though whispering, and Tom noticed that the red purse was on the table between them.

He frowned. He pushed through the door into the kitchen and saw a great big pile of dirty plates, pots and pans, stacked up beside the battered stone sink, waiting for his attention.

'Another day in paradise,' he muttered. He trudged over to the cooking range, lifted the heavy black kettle and carried it across to the sink. He tilted the kettle and hot water cascaded over the pots, sending clouds of steam billowing up into his face.

'You wash and I'll wipe,' said a familiar voice. He turned, staring in dull surprise. Cat smiled at him. 'Wassup?' she asked him. 'You look freaked.'

That was an understatement. He stared down at the kettle in his hand, which was suddenly much lighter, and saw that it was no longer a big, black iron affair, but a white plastic jug kettle with the word *Instaboil* printed on the side of it. He glanced around the room and somehow wasn't surprised to find he was no longer in Margaret's filthy stone kitchen, but a sleek, modern fitted one, complete with microwave, fan oven and pop-up toaster. He didn't recognise it. He was pretty sure it wasn't a place he'd been before and yet at the same time it seemed strangely familiar to him, as though he'd spent some time here.

He looked frantically around and saw a coaster lying on a worktop that said *I ♥ Manchester*. So he was back again? In front of him, above the sink, a double glazed window gave a view of a large, nicely tended garden below them, looking fresh and appealing in the sunshine. It was clearly an upstairs apartment they were in. But it wasn't the change of location that was the hardest thing to take in. It was Cat. She looked very different to how he remembered her.

For one thing, her hair was cut in a short, straight bob and she was wearing a splash of green makeup around her eyes. For another, she was dressed in modern clothing – blue jeans, Converse sneakers and a red T-shirt that said 'Party Girl.' Most puzzling of all, she looked about ten years older.

'Whoah!' said Tom. It seemed appropriate.

Fifteen

Cat gave him an odd look. 'What's the matter?' she asked him.

'Er . . . nothing,' he said. *Stay calm*, he told himself. *You've had things like this happen before. An alternative reality. Just go with it and eventually it'll sort itself out. It usually does.*

'What are you doing with the kettle?'

'Huh? Umm . . . Just getting some hot water?' he suggested.

Cat shook her head as though he were a hopeless case. 'For your information, there's this fantastic new invention,' she told him. She reached over and turned on the hot tap. 'See.'

He nodded and looked around until he found the base standing on a worktop. He went over and set the kettle down on it. 'I . . . didn't think the water would be hot enough,' he muttered.

'What? Not been paying the leccy bill again?' she teased him.

His mind was racing. He looked down at himself and saw he was wearing a check shirt, khaki combat trousers and black trainers. He'd never seen any of the clothes before, but they looked clean and tidy and, better still, they smelled ok. He looked around the open plan apartment. No sign of anybody else.

'Where's everyone else?' he murmured.

She glared at him. 'Everyone else?' she echoed. 'Like who?'

'My dad. Your mum?'

She gave him a wary look. 'Please tell me you haven't invited them over without telling me?' she growled.

'Er . . . no! No, of course not. I just . . .' He didn't know the best way to play this. He occupied himself for a moment, rubbing the washcloth across a couple of plates and handing them to Cat, who dried them with a tea towel and took them across to a cupboard. She seemed to know where everything went, so it was clear that she was no stranger here.

'So er . . . what happens when we finish this?' he wondered and now she gave him a look that made his heart race.

'Well, ' she said. 'You're going to listen to the next chapter of my masterpiece.' She smiled wickedly. 'After that, we'll see what happens.'

Tom noticed she still had a trace of the Scottish accent, though it seemed less broad than he remembered, as though she'd been living in Manchester a long while. 'So . . . er . . . what time do you have to go?' he wondered.

She stared at him. 'Go? Go where?'

'Haven't you somewhere you need to be?'

'Like where . . . for instance?'

He stared at her. 'Umm . . . Edinburgh?' he suggested.

She laughed. 'Funny man,' she said. She looked wistful. 'Edinburgh. I haven't been back since I was fourteen,' she said.

'But . . . how old are you now?' he protested.

She didn't answer, simply raised her eyebrows and he marvelled at how much older she looked. She must be in her early twenties he decided. He thought for a moment. Did that mean he was older too? He didn't *feel* any older.

'We keep saying we'll go up for the festival one year,' continued Cat. 'But something always comes up to stop us. Your flipping job.'

'My . . . job?'

'That bloody museum. It's always, "Ooh, Cat, we've got this new stuff arriving. I have to be there to oversee the Assyrian sculptures or whatever." I mean, everyone needs a holiday sometime.' She smiled at him. 'We really should go to Edinburgh. I think you'd love it there. And you've never been, have you?'

'Er . . . no,' lied Tom. 'No, never.' He knew from experience that it was always best to play along in these situations. 'That would be really cool, ' he said. 'Yeah, sure, let's do it.'

'This year?' she prompted him.

'Sure. Why not?' He handed her another plate and watched as she dried it. 'So, your dad,' he prompted. 'Is he still . . .?'

'Dead? Yeah, I'm afraid so.' She gave a snickering laugh. 'Sorry,' she said. 'Bad taste. What were you going to say?'

'Umm . . . I was going to say . . . is he still . . . on your mind and stuff?'

'No. It's so long ago now. You know, if it wasn't for old photographs I wouldn't even remember what he looked like.'

Tom frowned. Clearly Mr McCallum hadn't made it to this alternative reality. He was increasingly nervous of saying the wrong thing, but he still had a few more questions to ask. 'And . . . your mum?'

'Oh, she's fine, I think. Obsessed with this new diet she's on. She eats normally one day and then fasts the next. Sounds like nonsense to me. Well, you spoke to her yesterday on the phone. Didn't she *seem* ok?

'Oh, yeah. I think so. It's not like she needs to diet, is it?'

Cat frowned at him. 'We both thought she'd put on quite a bit at Christmas,' she said. 'And we *did* get her that exercise DVD.'

'Oh . . . yeah.' He stared into the washing up bowl. 'And . . . Fraser?'

Cat scowled. 'I'm *so* worried about him. I mean, what's happening? There hasn't been a word since his unit moved up to Helmand.'

Ok, thought Tom. *Helmand Province. Afghanistan.* So in this version of events, Fraser was in the army. It made perfect sense. He'd always loved messing around with his toy soldiers, though his current occupation was, of course, a good deal more serious than that.

'He'll be all right,' said Tom quietly. 'You know Fraser . . .'

She smiled, nodded. 'I couldn't believe that last FaceTime message he sent. Well, you saw him, he must have been a foot taller.' She went to the cupboard and slotted the plate in. 'I just want him to come home safe and sound.'

Tom moved the dishcloth around a last mug. 'I'm sure he'll be fine. And er . . . what about Jamie?' he wondered.

Cat lifted her head and looked puzzled. 'Who?'

'Er . . . Jamie. Daft Jamie. From Edinburgh?'

She shook her head. 'I haven't a clue who you're on about,' she told him. She frowned. 'Why do I feel like I'm being interviewed here?'

He tried a dismissive laugh and handed her the mug. 'Oh, sorry, I thought you knew him. He's just some kid who hangs around here. Talks with a stutter . . . walks with a limp?'

Cat shook her head. 'I think I'd remember somebody like *that*,' she said. She gave the mug a last wipe, carried it to the cupboard and put it away. 'All done,' she announced. She turned back. 'Now . . .' She put her arms around him and drew him close. 'I think we've got a bit of time before I need to crack on with the novel so . . .'

He felt himself colouring up. 'Whoah,' he said. 'Hey, time out! I'm not . . . I mean, I'm not . . . ready for this.'

She laughed at him. 'Ooh, excuse me, Mr Choosey.' She looked at him intently. 'Michael, what is wrong with you today?'

'Nothing, I just . . .' He broke off in surprise. 'Michael?' he said.

'Hmm?'

'You just called me Michael.'

'Yes. That was your name, last time I checked. Look, are you all right?'

'Er . . . sure, I'm fine, I just . . .'

A terrible thought had occurred to him. It was a crazy idea, but he couldn't seem to rid himself of it. Because something hadn't felt right from the moment he'd found himself here and it was simply that he felt *different*. He broke away from her and went out into the hallway where he somehow knew there was a full-length mirror. Cat trailed after him.

'Ok, I'm getting a little bit scared now.' she told him. 'You're being really weird.'

'I know . . . I just need to . . .' He broke off and stared at his reflection in the mirror. He didn't recognise the face looking back at him. He stood there, open-mouthed, gazing in stunned silence. The man in the mirror was taller and thinner and, Tom thought, several years older than he was. He had short black hair, a long thin face and what looked like dark stubble on his chin.

'Oh. My. God,' whispered Tom. He couldn't think of anything else to say.

Just then the doorbell rang at a volume that made him flinch.

'Who's that?' muttered Cat. 'Did you invite somebody over?'

Tom shook his head and in the mirror, the stranger's head shook back at him, perfectly synchronised. Cat trailed past him to the glass-fronted door. Tom turned to look at her and saw the dark silhouette of a figure standing on the other side of the glass. There was something horribly familiar about it.

'Cat,' he said. 'Wait . . .'

But her hand was already turning the latch and pulling the door open. Tom caught a glimpse of a dark figure in a brown leather cloak. Behind the bird-like mask a pair of eyes stared at Cat without a glint of humanity. One arm lifted and a gloved hand glittered with a flash of silver.

'CAT!' screamed Tom. And he was moving, moving towards the door, his arms outstretched to try and reach her in time, but suddenly, the hall seemed to be thirty feet long and the doorway was at the far end, an impossible distance away and he was already too late, too late to change anything. He saw the blade swing upwards into Cat's chest, saw her double over with a gasp of surprise, saw McSweeny's free arm close softly, almost tenderly around her shoulders. As Tom drew closer, he heard the muffled laughter behind the mask, hoarse, rasping, triumphant.

Then his own arms were around Cat, but she was folding, crumpling like tissue paper in his hands, crumbling away to nothing and the cloaked figure in the doorway shimmered and rippled as clouds of steam rose up to envelope it. A sudden whirling sensation filled Tom's head. There was a crashing sound which brought him abruptly back to reality.

He blinked and looked at his feet, where the remains of a large serving dish lay in fragments on the tiled floor of Margaret's kitchen.

'What's going on?' yelled a voice and Tom looked up in dull surprise. Margaret had just stalked into the room and was glaring at him indignantly. 'I told you to *wash* the dishes, not break them.'

Tom gestured at the fragments on the floor. 'It . . . slipped,' he said.

'Slipped, did it?' Margaret came forward and Tom noticed, with a jolt of alarm, that she had the length of rope in her hand. 'I'll teach you to be more careful,' she snarled and raised the rope to strike him. He lifted an arm to shield his face but the blow never came.

'Leave the boy alone!' Tom saw that Nell had just entered the room. She stood there in the doorway, glaring at Margaret, her expression steely. 'You lay one finger on him and you'll answer to me.'

Margaret turned and for a few moments the two women gazed at each other in mutual hatred. Then Margaret backed down. 'Clear that mess up,' she told Tom, and with that she strode past Nell, knocking her with her shoulder as she went by. The door slammed behind her.

Nell came over to Tom. 'Are you all right?' she asked him.

He nodded. He wasn't all right, but he could hardly explain why. He got down on his knees and started to pick up the shards of broken crockery. His hands were shaking. Nell got down beside him, to help.

'All that fuss over an old plate,' she murmured, shaking her head. 'Why, it's not worth a penny of anyone's money.'

Tom nodded. 'Thanks,' he said. He liked Nell. She seemed to be the only one who was really looking out for him. They dumped their respective fragments into a bin and got back to their feet. Nell looked at the huge pile of dishes piled in the sink and sighed. She found a filthy cloth and smiled at Tom.

'Here,' she said. 'You wash and I'll wipe.'

Sixteen

Tom woke with a gasp in the straw-filled stall, the stench of pigs in his nostrils and the chill grip of October all around him. He sat up, breathing heavily and once again, despite the cold, he was drenched in sweat. He'd been having a dream, a bad dream. And this time he was fairly certain it was a dream. He only had vague recollections of its content, but it had been something to do with Jamie. He'd seen the lad's pale face staring at him, his features arranged into an expression of pure terror. He'd been shouting something over and over, two words, Tom thought, but he couldn't remember what they were. Had it been . . . bird? And . . . hay? It didn't make any sense.

After a little while, he settled and managed to drag himself out of the straw. He went through his regular routine, giving himself a splash of icy water at the pump and collecting the bucket of scraps to feed to the pigs. It got to around the time when Jamie generally showed up but there was no sign of him this morning which was unusual – he was always so punctual. Tom remembered the row with Margaret the day before and figured he probably didn't feel like showing his face here until she'd calmed down a bit.

Hunger clawed at Tom's insides, so he let himself out of the back gate and walked along the close in search of Jamie. He was well-known in these parts and as he wandered along Tom asked the people he passed on the street if any of them had seen him that morning. None had.

Tom decided to try a few of the places that Jamie often visited. The obvious choice was the butcher; he knew Jamie called there every morning to ask for scraps, but the burly, red-faced man behind the counter hadn't seen him, which he himself said was very unusual.

'It's well past the time he usually calls,' said the man and he handed Tom scraps of cooked meat wrapped in waxed paper. 'I was saving these for him,' he said. 'Pass them on to him when you find him.'

Tom agreed, but he was so hungry he ate half of the meat as he walked along the street, knowing only too well that Jamie would have shared it with him anyway. When he had eaten exactly half of the contents he wrapped the rest up and stuffed the package into his pocket.

The woman who ran the fruit barrow hadn't seen Jamie either and she came up with a couple of soft, brown apples to pass on to him which Tom accepted gratefully. He ate one and put the other into his pocket. The woman at the cake shop told him she hadn't seen Jamie in days, but he only ever called there when he had money to spend and that wasn't very often. Annoyingly, the woman didn't offer Tom anything in the way of food and he left with a wistful look at the delicious tarts, puddings and pastries set out in the window.

He walked on along the close and spotted an elderly vagrant called Robert Kirkwood, who for some reason Jamie always called 'Bobby Awl.' He was a skinny, white-haired old fellow with a hacking cough. Tom knew he sometimes shared a sleeping spot with Jamie so he waved to him and stopped to talk.

'Hey, Bobby, have you seen Jamie today?

Bobby shook his head. 'I have not,' he said grumpily. 'I didn't see him last night, neither,' he said. 'Which is odd because he promised me he'd bring me a dram of whisky to warm me up.'

Tom frowned. 'Where would Jamie get the money for whisky?' he asked.

Bobby shrugged. 'I saw him around midday yesterday,' he explained. 'He told me he had a bit of a job lined up. Reckoned it would pay him sixpence.'

'What kind of a job?' asked Tom.

'He didn't say. Truth is, he was kind of secretive about it.' Bobby scratched his stubbled chin. 'Shame. I was looking forward to that drink. It was cold last night.' And with that he gave a loud cough and shuffled on his way, his filthy coat clutched tight around him.

Tom carried on along the close, but he was beginning to get very concerned about Jamie. He couldn't help thinking about the dream he'd had, although try as he might, he couldn't put the broken pieces together. It was like the plate he'd dropped in Margaret's kitchen, the jagged shards scattered across the tiled floor.

Just then he saw Billy strolling towards him, his pipe in his mouth, his hands in his pockets. He smiled amiably when he saw Tom and pulled the pipe out of his mouth. 'What are you doing out so early?' he asked.

'I was going to ask you the same question,' said Tom. He couldn't help noticing that Billy had a purple bruise over one eye and a swollen lip. 'What happened to you?' he asked.

'Ah, 'tis nothin'. Me and Will had a disagreement over money. He seemed to think I owed him, but the way I saw it, 'twas the other way around. Anyhow, he got the worst of it, I'd say.' He shook his head. 'Anyway, it's the last straw. Me and Nell are moving out and this time we aren't coming back.'

'Moving out?' Tom didn't like the sound of that. Without Billy and Nell around, Laird's was going to be even grimmer. 'Going to stay with your brother again?'

'No, we've found ourselves a nice little place, just a stone's throw from here.' He noted Tom's glum expression and grinned. 'Don't worry, we'll still be doing our drinking at Laird's. You'll see plenty of us.'

Tom nodded, feeling a little reassured. 'Billy, you haven't seen Jamie anywhere, have you?'

Billy shook his head. 'I haven't,' he said. 'Why do you ask?'

'I'm getting worried about him. He didn't turn up this morning and I know he had a big row with Margaret yesterday.'

'Is that right?' Billy rolled his eyes. 'Him and the rest of Edinburgh, I'd say. That woman could argue with a paper bag if she put her mind to it. That's another reason why we're moving out.'

'I heard Jamie had a job somewhere last night. You wouldn't know anything about that, would you?'

Billy shrugged. 'He works for all kinds of people,' he said. 'I don't keep an eye what he does.' He thought for a moment. 'You know, that lad is a vagabond at heart. He doesn't stay in the one place for very long. I wouldn't be at all surprised if he's moved on for the winter.'

'Moved on?'

'Sure. When the weather gets colder he often heads down to Leith. I believe he has relatives there.'

'He's never mentioned them to me,' said Tom. 'And I don't think he'd leave without saying goodbye.'

'Ah, Daft Jamie is a law unto himself,' said Billy. 'I wouldn't worry, that boy might act like a halfwit, but he well knows how to take care of his own business. Well, must get moving. I've got some people coming over to move our stuff across to the new place.' He winked. 'No rest for the wicked,' he said. 'Don't you be going missing, now, if Margaret comes lookin' for ya. Without Nell around to fight your corner, she'll be calling the tune and you'll be the one doing the dancing.' He strolled on along the street, whistling tunelessly.

Tom gazed after him for a moment. He knew that Margaret might well be looking for him with a list of menial tasks for his attention, and he knew how angry she could be if she couldn't find him. But at the same time he didn't feel inclined to head back just yet. Instead, he went to the McCallum's house. He rapped

162

on the door and after a few moments Mary appeared, smiling warmly.

'Tom,' she said. 'We haven't seen you in a while.' She seemed puzzled. 'On your own today?'

He nodded. 'I can't find Jamie,' he said. 'I've been asking around, but nobody's seen him.'

'That's strange. Well, come along inside.' He stepped into the hall and she studied him for a moment. 'I'd say they aren't keeping you very clean at that lodging house,' she observed. 'What say I get some water and fill the tin bath for you in the kitchen?'

'Really?' Tom was delighted at the idea. 'Oh, that would be cool.'

'No, it would be *hot*,' she corrected him. 'I'll heat it on the stove. And those clothes look like they could do with a good wash. Maybe I could hunt out some of the things that Fraser has grown out of, just until your own clothes are ready. What do you think?'

'Thanks, Mary. I really appreciate it.'

She smiled. 'You're more than welcome. Why don't you go up and see Cat and Fraser?' she suggested. 'I'll call you when your bath's ready.'

He found them in the attic room, seated at their table, industrious as ever. Cat was sewing something, but she smiled welcomingly when Tom came in and set the fabric down. At least she seemed to have forgiven him for the incident at the Grassmarket. After his recent meeting with an altogether different Cat, it seemed strange to see her back in her nineteenth-century attire.

Fraser kept his head down over something he was working on.

'Tom!' said Cat. 'It's been ages. No Jamie today?'

He explained the situation. 'Billy thinks he might have gone to stay with some relatives in Leith,' said Tom.

'Really?' Cat frowned. 'He's never mentioned relatives to me. I'm sure he wouldn't leave Edinburgh, though. For one thing, his mother is here.'

'But they don't get on,' reasoned Tom.

'They don't, but at the same time, blood is thicker than water. He still calls to see her. He just doesn't *stay* there.'

'I suppose I could try talking to his mum. Does she live near here?'

'Oh yes, not so far away. I could take you there later if you like.'

Tom nodded. 'It's worth a try,' he said.

Cat was now looking at Tom's filthy clothing. She frowned, wrinkling her nose. 'Don't they have a bath at the lodging house?' she asked.

'Margaret's too mean with the water,' said Tom. 'But Mary is going to let me have a bath here.' He looked at Fraser. 'She said I could wear some of your old clothes, if that's ok?'

Fraser grunted. 'Suit yourself,' he said. He was intent on whatever he was doing, the tip of his tongue protruding from his lips as he worked on something delicate with his sharp, hooked knife.

Tom moved closer. 'What are you making?'

164

Fraser leaned back a little. 'It was your idea, really.'

Tom stared. 'Oh,' he said. Fraser was making a little coffin.

'I admit, it seemed like a daft idea when you first mentioned it,' he said. 'But the more I thought about it, the more I couldn't get it out of my head.' He picked up one of the little dressed dolls and placed it into the open coffin where it fitted snugly. He showed Tom the lid of the coffin which was decorated with pieces of crudely cut tin. 'I made these decorations from some old shoe buckles,' he said. 'What do you think?'

'It's . . . fantastic,' he said. 'How . . . how many are you going to make?'

Fraser shrugged. 'I've made three, so far,' he said. 'I'm thinking of it as a symbolic burial for the dead soldiers of Culloden.'

'You'd need to make an awful lot of coffins to accommodate them all,' said Cat. She pointed to the pile of fabric. 'I'm making wee suits for them. Fraser still won't let me put dresses on any of them.'

'I should think not,' said Fraser sternly. 'Soldiers in dresses! What an idea.'

Cat made a face at her brother, but he didn't notice. He went back to his carving, moving the hooked knife with great care.

Tom stood there, trying to get his head around what had just happened. He'd seen the mysterious coffins in the National Museum and he'd read how scholars had been speculating for years about the possible meaning of them. Now he'd come back in time and it seemed he'd given the idea of making them to Fraser. Which meant . . . if he'd got it right in his mind, that without him coming back, the coffins would never have existed in the first place. Which was mind-boggling.

'Weird,' he muttered.

'What's weird?' asked Cat.

'I can't . . . it's too . . .' He shook his head, dismissed the idea. He looked at Cat. 'You remember what I told you that day at the Grassmarket? About where I came from and everything?'

She nodded warily. 'I remember,' she said.

'Have you had a chance to think about it?' He glanced uncertainly at Fraser. 'Does he . . .?'

'I told him what you said.'

'And?'

'I told her you were a lunatic,' said Fraser matter-of-factly. 'And that you should probably be locked up for your own safety and the safety of others.' He smiled. 'No offence,' he added.

'None taken,' Tom assured him. 'Cat?'

She sighed. 'I thought about it very hard,' she told him. 'I weighed up the evidence. You arrived here and you weren't like anybody else I'd ever met. You dressed differently, you talked differently. Then I remembered when we were asking you questions about how long it took you to get here. You kept changing your story, almost as though you were saying what we expected to hear. First it was hours then it was one day, two days, three days . . .'

Tom looked straight into her eyes.

'Cat, I swear to you, this is the God's honest truth. I came from Manchester to Edinburgh on a modern train. Not like the old steam trains you've seen, its faster and quieter. It took me three hours to get from Manchester to Edinburgh.'

There was a deep silence while they considered this. Even Fraser was moved to stop working for a moment. 'Three hours?' he echoed.

'Well, three hours and fifteen minutes, if you must know.'

Fraser laughed dismissively. 'That's ridiculous,' he said. 'You can't expect us to believe that.'

'Ok.' Tom reached into his pocket and pulled out his mobile phone. 'See this? It's called a mobile phone. It's not working at the moment because it's out of power. But if it *was* working I could use this to talk to people all over the world, instantly. I could take your photograph with it . . . that's like a perfect likeness of you? I could send emails, text messages, I could play music on it . . .'

Fraser reached out a hand and took the phone from him. 'This is a black box,' he said, tapping the glass with his finger.

'Yeah, it is, but you need to see it working! Only I can't charge it because I've no power lead and even if I had one, there's no such thing as electricity yet. See, in the future there won't be gas lamps and stuff. You just flick a switch and the lights come on . . .' Fraser was looking at him blankly.

'It just . . . wait.' Tom reached into his pocket and pulled out the two ten pound notes he'd carried since he first arrived. 'Look at this money,' he said. He handed them a note each. 'See that woman, that's the Queen of England. Not now, but in the future. And look, on the other side? This bearded guy. That's Charles Darwin. Look at the dates . . .'

'1809 to 1882,' said Fraser, flatly. 'I know of a Charles Darwin. Our University professor told me about him. He reckons he's an idiot. He was studying medicine under Dr Munro, here in Edinburgh, but he threw it all up in the second year and moved to England to study natural history, of all things.' Fraser laughed dismissively. 'Ruined a promising career. But he's only young, he didn't have a big beard like this fellow.'

'Yes, that's because it's a picture of him when he's an old man. 1882 is when he's going to die. How . . . how could I know that if I wasn't from the future?'

Fraser smiled. 'Come back in fifty-two years and we'll see if you're right,' he suggested. 'This isn't proof of anything, Tom. It's just two dates on a scrap of paper.'

'I believe him,' said Cat and Tom could have hugged her.

'Och, if he told you he was from the moon, you'd believe him,' said Fraser, dismissively. 'He'll be telling us next that people have travelled *there*.'

'They *have*,' Tom assured him. 'But that's old news to me. That happened back in the sixties.'

'Men went to the moon?' muttered Fraser and now he looked really worried.

'That's not important right now. See, when this thing happens to me . . . when I travel through time, it's like I've got no control over it. And the thing is, I could just go back to my own time without any warning.'

Cat looked desolate. 'What do you mean, 'just go back?''

'Exactly what I say. One minute I'd be here and the next . . .' He snapped his fingers. 'Gone.'

'But you'd come back again?'

'Probably not. I wouldn't have any control over it. I mean, I keep going back anyway, just for a short while, but when I do, everything's different and there's this guy from the seventeenth century, William McSweeny, and he's chasing me. I mean, I don't how he's doing it, but he's there. And just yesterday, Cat, I went back for a while and *you* were there, only you weren't you exactly and I . . . I was some guy called Michael.'

'Oh, well, we've all done that from time to time,' said Fraser, and Cat shot a scathing look at him.

'Wheesht,' she said.

'No, I understand,' said Tom, 'I know it sounds crazy.' He frowned, but went on with what he needed to say. 'I just wanted to tell you . . . *both* of you, that if it does happen . . . if I suddenly go back to my own time, it won't be because I *want* to, ok?'

'Maybe that's what's happened to Jamie,' said Fraser. 'Perhaps he's gone back in time or forward in time, or whatever it is you do.'

Tom shook his head. 'I don't think so,' he said. 'I think something bad might have happened to him. I dreamed about him last night . . .'

'What kind of dream?' asked Cat.

'I don't remember much about it. Just that he was scared and he kept shouting something to me . . . but it doesn't make any sense. I think he was saying 'bird' And . . . 'hay'?'

Cat and Fraser glanced at each other as though they recognised something.

'What?' asked Tom.

'It probably doesn't mean anything,' said Cat.

'It's a song,' said Fraser. 'A daft wee song we used to sing every morning at the sessional school.'

'How does it go?'

Cat thought for a moment and then sang, in a quavering little voice.

'*The bird in the hay, one bright summer's day*
He sang as he flew o'er the meadow.
Oh can't you all see, that I'm healthy and free
And I'm such a handsome young fellow.'

Fraser took up the refrain in his deeper tone.

'*My feathers are green, with a beautiful sheen*
and my beak is a splendid bright yellow.
I look down on the world, with my feathers unfurled
And I sing in a voice deep and mellow.'

Now they sang the chorus together.

'*Hey diddly dee, hey diddly dum, hey diddly diddly*
dorum . . .'

They broke off, looking slightly embarrassed.

'That's as much as I can remember,' said Fraser. 'I used to hate that song.'

'Hmm.' Tom thought about it. 'I can't see why Jamie would want me to tell me about that,' he said. 'A song.'

'And not a very good one at that,' said Fraser. 'Och, perhaps it doesn't mean anything. Perhaps it was just a dream. Some dreams are just nonsense.'

Just then Mary called from downstairs. 'Tom. Your bath's ready.'

He looked from Cat to Fraser and back again. 'Mary,' he said. 'What does she think about the time travel business?'

There was a brief silence. Then Cat said, 'She thinks you're . . .'

'Yes?'

'She thinks you're gone in the head,' said Fraser, helpfully. 'She thinks you're as crazy as a long-tailed cat in a room full of rocking chairs.'

'Oh . . . right. Well, I don't suppose I can blame her.' Tom shrugged. 'I'll go and have that bath,' he said. As he started to turn away Cat stepped forward and put her arms around him.

'I believe you,' she whispered fiercely. 'I hope that helps.'

'It does,' he assured her. 'Lots.'

He felt a sudden impulse to kiss her, but he was uncomfortably aware that Fraser was studying him frostily, so he pulled away from her, gave her a last smile and went down the stairs to the kitchen, where, once Mary had left him in privacy, he removed his reeking clothes and had what must have been the most enjoyable bath of his entire life.

Seventeen

Tom and Cat made their way through the maze of narrow streets that branched off from Tanner's close. Tom felt vaguely ridiculous, dressed in Fraser's ill-fitting cast-offs; a pair of tweedy trousers, a collarless shirt and a moleskin jacket, but at least he was clean and smelled better than he had in ages. He wasn't sure if Jamie's mother would be able to tell him anything useful, but he knew he had to speak to her just the same. They walked for some time in silence. Then:

'This is the place,' said Cat.

Tom gazed at the ramshackle little house doubtfully. It made the other dwellings on the close look luxurious by comparison. It was badly dilapidated, the walls green with mould, the single window coated in a thick layer of grime. Tom stepped up to knock on the rotten wooden doorway and it swung open under his touch. He looked at Cat.

'Why isn't it locked?' he asked her.

'Mrs Wilson always leaves the door open,' she told him. 'She's bad on her feet, so she prefers to let people come and go as they please.'

'That's not very safe,' said Tom.

'Well, who would want to harm an old lady?' asked Cat and Tom looked at her disbelievingly. He couldn't imagine anybody from his day and age who would dream of taking a risk like that. He remembered something that Nell had said to him − *Don't be too trusting. People aren't always what they seem.*

He stepped into a gloomy, damp-smelling hallway and called out.

'Hello? Anyone at home?'

'In here,' croaked a voice and he and Cat walked along the hall to another door and pushed it open. It was dark in there, only a thin wash of daylight seeping in through the filthy windowpane and it took a few moments for his eyes to adjust. Then he was able to make out the hunched figure of an old woman sitting in a chair in the corner of a bare and cheerless little room. A pathetic fire smouldered in a cast iron grate but it seemed no warmer in the room than it had been outside.

'Mrs Wilson?' asked Tom, walking forward. 'Is that you?'

'Who wants to know?' asked the woman and now Tom could make out her face. It was pale and wizened with age and the tiny eyes that gazed steadfastly back at him were grey and watery. She was wrapped in a thick blanket which came up over her head and shoulders. A white clay pipe jutted from her mouth, emitting clouds of aromatic smoke, and her veined hands rested on the handle of a stout black stick. She looked impossibly old, Tom thought, but realised that living in a place like this would age a person prematurely. In reality, she might be no older than sixty or seventy years.

He moved closer still and Cat went with him, taking hold of his hand as she did so, as though being in the presence of the woman was making her nervous. 'My name's Tom Afflick and this is Cat . . . er, Catriona McCallum.'

'Ah, the McCallum girl.' Mrs Wilson nodded and seemed to relax a little. 'I know you,' she said. 'I know your mother. She's a good enough woman, by all accounts.' Her gaze flicked across to Tom. 'You, I don't know.'

'We're friends of Jamie,' said Tom.

'Are you now?' Mrs Wilson took the pipe out of her mouth. 'Well, then, perhaps you might be able to tell me what's happened to him and why he hasn't been to see his poor widowed mother in two whole days.'

'Umm. Well, that's just the thing,' said Tom. 'We haven't seen him either. We're looking for him.'

'Does he owe you money?' asked Mrs Wilson. 'Because if that's what this is about, you've come to the wrong place. I'm just an old woman without so much as a farthing to my name.'

'Oh, it's nothing like that,' Cat assured her. 'We're worried about him, that's all.'

'I see him every morning,' explained Tom. 'Without fail. We eat breakfast together. Only he didn't turn up today and I talked to a friend of his called Bobby Awl, who said he was expecting to see Jamie last night, but he didn't show up there, either.'

Mrs Wilson's eyes narrowed. 'You'll be the English

boy Jamie was telling me about,' she said. 'The one he has such a high opinion of.'

'Oh . . . I wouldn't know about that,' said Tom. 'We're just mates, you know? But we look out for each other. When did you last see him?'

'The day before yesterday.' She shook her head. 'It's not like him, this. He calls to see me every day of the week, to make sure I'm all right.'

Tom was surprised to hear this. Jamie rarely said much about his mother and when he did, it was generally a complaint about her brutal treatment of him. Hadn't he said something about being beaten for eating a loaf of bread?

'I didn't know he came so often,' admitted Tom.

'Of course he does. And who do you think washes his clothes for him? That boy would be like a destitute if I didn't take care of it.'

'He told Bobby Awl that he had some kind of job to do last night. He didn't mention that to you, when you last saw him?'

Mrs Wilson gave a wry smile. 'Ah, he wouldn't be telling me about a thing like that. Not if there was money involved. He knows I'd soon be after him for a share of it.' She sucked on her pipe for a moment, blowing out more smoke. 'It's not easy surviving at my time of life. I only have Jamie. Oh, I've a daughter, but I don't see much of her. She's far too busy with her fancy friends to spend time on the likes of me.'

'Umm . . . what about your relatives in Leith?' asked Tom.

Mrs Wilson stared at him. 'I don't know anyone in Leith,' she told him. 'If we've got relatives there, it's news to me.'

'Oh but, I thought . . .'

'You thought wrong boy. I don't know why Jamie would tell you that.'

'It wasn't Jamie,' said Tom. He frowned. So Billy had been lying about that. But why, what possible reason could he have? Unless he knew something about Jamie's disappearance. Unless he was somehow involved . . . He decided that he was going to have a long talk with Billy just as soon as he got back to Laird's.

'Can you think of any other reason why Jamie might want to leave Edinburgh?' he asked.

Mrs Wilson laughed. 'Jamie could no more leave this city than he could dance a Highland fling,' she said. 'He's born and bred here and never stepped out of the place his entire life.' Her expression changed to a look of misery. 'Something's happened to him,' she said with total conviction. 'I know it! Haven't I always told him his curiosity would get him into trouble one day? He's probably been robbed, murdered, I shouldn't wonder.'

'We don't know that,' said Cat. She let go of Tom's hand and moved forward to crouch down in front of the old woman. 'I'm sure there's some explanation,' she said. 'Everybody loves Jamie, nobody would want to harm him.'

Mrs Wilson scoffed at that. 'You're a naïve girl

if you believe that,' she said bluntly. 'Edinburgh's changed. It used to be kinder to the old than it is now. People like myself were given respect. But bad things are happening lately. I've heard rumours . . .'

'What kind of rumours?' asked Tom, intrigued.

'About people going missing. There was Effie who used to sell scraps of leather around the close. She vanished overnight. And then the Haldane's. First the mother and then the daughter. Just up and disappeared they did and nobody seems to have the least idea what might have happened to them.' She leaned over and spat onto the floor. 'You mark my words, something's going on around Tanner's Close and it's the devil's work. It'll be me next. There'll be nobody to miss me if Jamie's gone.'

Tom stood there, looking at the old woman and wishing there was something he could say to cheer her up. But he was beginning to think that she was right and the more he thought about it, the more he realised that it had something to do with Billy and Will. He remembered meeting Peggy Haldane, that time she'd turned up looking for her mother. Margaret had been as nice as pie to her and had led her away for a drink of brandy. And that very evening, he and Jamie had been hired to make a second delivery to the Surgeons' Hall. He looked at Cat. 'We should go,' he said. 'I need to have a talk with Billy.'

'Shall I come with you?' she asked.

Tom shook his head. 'I think I'd better do this on

my own.' He looked back to Mrs Wilson. 'Thanks,' he said. 'If I hear anything about Jamie, I'll come and let you know.'

'I'd appreciate it,' said the old woman.

Tom suddenly felt terribly sorry for her. He had the distinct impression that Jamie wasn't coming back. He reached into his pocket and took out what was left of the money he'd been paid for making the two deliveries to Surgeons' Hall. He stepped forward and pressed it into the old woman's hand. 'It's not much,' he said, 'but it's all I've got.'

'Bless you,' she said. 'You're very kind.'

Tom shrugged. They said their goodbyes and let themselves out of the damp old house. They walked slowly back to the McCallum's.

'Why do you need to talk to Billy?' asked Cat.

'Because he knows something,' said Tom. 'He's told me lies about Jamie.'

'Lies? Why would he do that?'

'Because I think he knows more than he's letting on.'

She reached out and squeezed his hand. 'Be careful,' she warned him.

'I will,' he promised her.

After dropping Cat off at the McCallums, he made an excuse and headed back towards Laird's, walking with some urgency. Since he wouldn't stay to eat, Mary made him a sandwich and presented him with his damp washing in a cloth bag, telling him to peg it out to dry somewhere. Tom ate the sandwich as he walked along, but he was barely aware of the taste because now, a whole series of questions were whirling around in his head, questions that urgently needed answering. There were so many unexplained things that had happened to him since he'd arrived here, and he'd taken so much on trust, because he genuinely liked Billy and had been charmed by his confident, affable manner. He'd accepted the story about the deliveries of dodgy beef up to the Surgeons' Hall but now he wondered if there was something else in those tightly-nailed packing cases, something more sinister. What had really happened to the Haldanes? Why had Margaret pretended that Peggy's purse belonged to her? And most damning of all, why had Billy lied about Jamie having relatives in Leith?

Tom was striding along, concentrating furiously and at first he didn't notice that he seemed to be speeding up, moving faster and faster along the street. Then a man passed by him in a blur of movement, going so fast that Tom couldn't really make out any details. He realised his speed was increasing, second by second and he made a conscious effort to slow himself down, but he simply couldn't do it. His feet seemed to have a life of their own, covering the ground beneath him at an incredible pace and now it seemed to him that he was running, he was running faster than he had ever run in his entire life, faster than even seemed humanly possible, the other people on the street whizzing past him like briefly glimpsed phantoms. His head began to fill with that familiar whirling sensation.

Oh no, he thought, *not now*! But he was powerless to do anything but surrender to what was happening to him, the world whizzing past like an adrenalin-fuelled carnival ride, a maelstrom of stomach-lurching sound and colour.

Suddenly he came to a halt, so abrupt that he gasped to catch his breath. A face was looking at him; a round inhuman face with cut-out eyes, triangular slit nostrils and a jagged grinning mouth, all of which seemed to glow with an eerie, supernatural light.

'What do you think?' asked Billy. He was holding a knife and he was smiling at Tom, his clay pipe clenched between his teeth. 'That should scare the very life out of 'em, don'tcha think?'

Eighteen

Tom stared stupidly around. He was back in the stable and it was evening. The only light came from an oil lamp and the flickering candle inside the Hallowe'en lantern that Billy had just finished carving. As Tom looked on he made a few last minute adjustments to it, working the sharp knife into the large hollowed-out turnip with well-practised ease. Tom looked down at himself. He was back in his regular clothes which seemed slightly cleaner than when he had last seen them, though they had already lost the just-washed freshness that he would have expected them to have. He struggled to find words and Billy gave him an odd look. 'What's up with you?' he asked. 'Cat got your tongue?'

'Umm . . . er . . .' Tom waved his hands, trying to find appropriate words. 'I . . . I thought you said you were moving out of Laird's?'

'I did. Weeks ago. I still come back here to drink though.' He winked. 'I like the company.' He studied Tom for a moment. 'Are you all right? You seem . . . a little unsettled.'

Tom could only point stupidly at the lantern. 'What's that in aid of?' he asked dismally.

'It's for the party,' said Billy. 'Sure, it isn't a proper All Hallow's Night without a Jack-O-Lantern.'

'All Hallow's Night?' muttered Tom. 'That means it's . . . October the thirty first?' he said.

'They don't get much past you,' observed Billy.

Tom realised that time had jumped on again. When he'd set off from Cat's it had been the middle of October. He had lost two weeks in a matter of moments. He still felt dizzy and confused and had no way of knowing what had happened in the time he'd lost.

'Oh, when I was a lad,' said Billy cheerfully, 'we had some great Samhain parties, so we did. We'd do all the games, you know? Ducking for apples, hiding rings in a bowl of colcannon. And then me and the other lads of the village, we'd take off and we'd play tricks on all the farmers round about us. Afterwards, we'd have ghost stories. They'd tell us all about Stingy Jack and the Banshee and the Pooka. We'd go to bed terrified, so we would, and we'd lie awake the whole night, listening for the wail of the banshee, convinced that she would come for one of us that very night.' He chuckled. 'Me and some friends – one time, we were convinced we'd seen the Pooka. A big black dog, it was, with eyes that glowed like hot coals . . . I tell you what, we ran home and dived into our beds and pulled the covers up over our heads . . .' His voice trailed off. 'They were good times,' he said. 'So I said to Nell. Tonight we'll have ourselves a real Hallowe'en party. Never mind all them disapproving Protestant Scots! Margaret didn't want to do it, of course. She said it was godless and inviting the devil to come and claim us.

But Will managed to persuade . . .' He stopped talking and looked at Tom. 'Are you all right, boy? You look as though you've seen Stingy Jack yourself.'

'I need to talk to you,' said Tom, making an attempt to gather his wits about him. 'About Jamie.'

Billy looked weary. 'That again?' he complained. 'Sure, I thought I explained everything to you.'

'Did you?' Tom frowned. 'I . . . I don't remember.'

'Ah, sure you do! That business about me, thinking he had relatives in Leith? Is that what you're talking about?'

'Er . . . yes. That's exactly it. Why . . .? I don't understand why you lied to me about it.'

Billy sighed. 'I didn't lie. It was just something I was told. But you remember, in the end, I decided maybe I'd got him mixed up with one of those other n'er-do-wells he used to hang about with.' Billy frowned. 'Look, lad, I know the two of you was close, but what happened to Jamie could have happened to any young lad that spent his nights sleeping rough. I don't know how many times I told him to get some shoes on his feet and find himself somewhere warm to spend the night. But he wouldn't listen to any of us . . .'

'Wait! What do you mean, "what happened to Jamie?" He's . . . he's just missing . . . isn't he?'

Billy looked awkward. 'I thought you knew,' he said. 'Wasn't it me that broke the news to you in the first place?'

'What news?' persisted Tom.

Billy frowned. 'Jamie's, dead, boy. Somebody up at the Surgeons' Hall recognised his body. They think he must have frozen to death.'

Tom stared at Billy, his mouth open. 'Dead?' he croaked. 'No, you . . . you must be mistaken. He can't be . . .' Tom didn't even want to say the word again, because that would make it real.

Billy shook his head. 'They're pretty sure it was him. Trouble is, by the time those damned surgeons had been at work on him, it was hard to tell. He'd been, what do they call it? Dissected.' He grimaced, shook his head. 'Lad, I don't understand. You *knew* all this. Sure, didn't I come and tell you the moment I heard the bad news?'

Tom's vision blurred as his eyes filled with tears. He had feared something like this, had even suspected as much. But to be told about it, weeks after the event, as though it was common knowledge? It was too much. He wondered if the McCallums knew. Grief overcame him and he began to cry. Billy came over and put a comforting arm around his shoulders.

'Now then, don't take on, so. Jamie wouldn't have wanted you to cry for him, like that. Poor simple soul that he was, he . . .'

'He wasn't simple!' snapped Tom, angrily. 'He was clever. He was one of the cleverest guys I ever met. And one of the kindest.'

Billy nodded. 'I meant no offence,' he said. 'Really.' He waved a hand at the lantern. 'Ah, come on,' he said, 'What say we take this inside and raise a glass or two to Jamie's memory? He wouldn't want to see you standing there blubbing over him like that.'

'But . . . we can't just . . .'

'Sure we can! Come on, we'll go in.' Billy stepped away from him and lifted the turnip in both hands. 'The ould gang's waiting for us in there. Will . . . Nell. She's there. You can talk to her about it.' He started towards the doorway and Tom had no real option but to follow, even though he had never felt more like being alone. They crossed the darkened yard. A huge full moon hung in the cloudless sky, gazing serenely down on them and it was bitterly cold.

They went in through the back entrance and along the corridor to the main room. Billy pushed open the door and Tom saw at once that the place was packed with cheery, raucous drinkers. In one corner of the room a group of children had a barrel filled with water and were bobbing for apples. Others apples were strung from a line and the taller children were trying to take bites out of them, their hands clasped behind their backs. The grey-haired fiddle player was sawing out one of his discordant jigs on the makeshift stage and the audience were clapping their hands and stamping their feet in time to the music. There was a big cheer as Billy strode into the room and lifted the turnip above his head so every one could see it. 'Here's Stingy Jack,' he roared. 'Now the party can really begin.'

He set the turnip down on the bar, had a quick word with Margaret and then led Tom through the crowds up to the top table. Will and Nell were in their usual places and Tom saw that there were other people sitting there too, a middle aged couple, who sat either side of Will and a grey-haired old lady who was chatting to Nell and drinking eagerly from a large mug of whisky.

'Find a seat for this young feller,' shouted Billy and a wooden chair was brought and set down beside Billy's. Nell looked across at Tom with evident concern.

'Tom, what's the matter?' she asked him. 'You look like you've been crying.'

'Ah, he was just thinking on young Jamie,' said Billy, settling down beside her. 'I thought he'd already come to terms with it, but he's feeling it bad tonight.'

Nell reached past the old woman and squeezed Tom's hand. 'We don't know for sure it was him,' she said. 'It seems some young doctor thought he recognised him when the body was first brought in, but by the time anybody got there to have a look, he'd been . . .' She grimaced. 'Well, you know. They couldn't properly identify what was left. He could turn up yet. Don't lose hope.'

Tom nodded, but at the moment, hope seemed out of reach.

Margaret trudged over with a tray of drinks and set them down on the table. She had the usual disapproving expression on her face.

'Ah, don't look like that, Margaret,' said Billy. 'Tonight of all nights, you should be happy. You and all the other ould witches!'

There was laughter at the table although Margaret

clearly didn't find the remark in the least bit funny. She glared at him and stalked away.

'Ah, come on!' he shouted after her. 'Sure, I was only kiddin' ya.'

'Leave it,' advised Will. 'Let her stew.' He studied Tom for a moment. 'Give the boy a strong drink,' he suggested.

Billy placed a mug of whisky in front of Tom. 'There now,' he said. 'Get that inside you. You'll feel better.'

Tom didn't have the strength to resist. He lifted the mug to his lips and took a gulp. The liquid seemed to blossom like fire as it went down and he couldn't stop himself from coughing.

'That's the spirit!' yelled Billy and slapped him hard on the back. 'Come on now, we'll have no long faces tonight. Jamie had no time for that kind of thing. Tom, let me introduce you to some new people.' He indicated the couple next to Will. 'This is James and Ann Gray, who have been lodging over at my place for a few days. They're moving on tonight, so we invited 'em to our little get-together.'

The Grays nodded and raised their drinks, prompting Tom to have another sip, vile though it was.

'Good health to you,' said Mr Gray.

Now Billy indicated the old lady. 'And this lovely creature is Mrs Mary Docherty, who I met in the Grassmarket today and who I believe may be a relation of mine. Sure, wasn't Docherty my mother's maiden name?'

The old woman directed a gap-toothed grin at Tom.

'De-lighted,' she said. 'Sure, any friend of Billy's is a good friend of mine!' She had a strong Irish accent and it was clear from her slurred words that she had already drunk more than was good for her. She insisted on knocking her mug of whisky against Tom's with such force that liquid splashed all over Billy's lap, but he just laughed and urged her to drink up because she had another mug waiting for her.

Tom sat there, desolate, as the party rattled on around him. He reminded himself of what Nell had said, that maybe the body hadn't been Jamie's, but somehow, he couldn't find much hope within him. If several weeks had gone by and there'd been no sign of Jamie then surely something bad had happened to him. And he couldn't stop thinking about what Billy had said. Jamie's body had turned up at the Surgeons' Hall – the very place that Tom had visited on two separate occasions. Surely that had to be more than a coincidence.

As the hours rolled by and the drinking intensified it quickly became clear that Mrs Docherty had had more than enough. Her skinny body began flopping this way and that, and her occasional comments became increasingly incoherent. At one point she attempted to sing an old Irish song, but she conked out halfway through it and her head slumped onto her chest. Billy looked at Nell.

'I think Mrs Docherty's ready for her bed,' he observed. 'Nell, why don't you take her over to our place and make her comfortable in our room? I'll be along in a little while.' Tom noticed that an intense look flashed between Billy and Nell, as though she was momentarily defying him over something, although she nodded obediently and helped the old woman out of her chair. She threw one of Mrs Docherty's arms across her shoulder and led her away from the table, and through the midst of the crowd towards the exit.

'I reckon she'll sleep well enough,' observed Will, with that sardonic smile of his. His raised his mug of whiskey. 'To sound sleepers,' he said and everybody drank. Billy laughed as if at some private joke. It was clear that he too was pretty drunk. He reached into the pocket of his waistcoat and took out a brass snuffbox. He flipped it open and taking a copper spoon out of it, lifted a pinch of snuff to his nose and inhaled deeply.

Tom stared at him. 'Where did you get that?' he snapped, in a voice so loud, that everyone at the table turned to look.

'Wha'?' grunted Billy.

'That snuffbox. It looks like Jamie's.'

Billy sneered. 'Ah, don't talk daft, boy. This is mine.' Billy attempted to put the spoon back into the box, but Tom was already up out of his chair, leaning forward to make a grab for it, scattering clouds of snuff in all directions.

'What's got into you?' snarled Billy. 'Have you gone mad?'

Tom had the spoon now and had turned it upside

down to reveal seven little holes punched into the handle.

'This *is* Jamie's!' he yelled. 'What are you . . . what are you doing with it?'

'Ah, sure, he gave it to me before he left,' said Billy, waving a hand as though it was nothing.

'No way. He wouldn't do that!' Tom looked around in disbelief. 'Why has Billy got –?'

His words were cut off as Billy grabbed him by the lapels of his jacket and pulled him down hard, into the seat next to his. He leaned in close, still smiling, affable as ever. 'I'd advise you to lower your voice,' he said quietly, his own heavy with menace. 'Or I'll be obliged to lower it for you.'

Tom stared at him in disbelief. It was as though Billy had been wearing a mask and it had just slipped to reveal an entirely different face beneath. 'But Billy, Jamie wouldn't have given that to anyone, it was his most favourite thing in the world.'

'And I'm tellin' ya, that he *did* give it to me, so let that be the end of it.'

Tom struggled, but Billy's powerful hand kept him in the chair.

Now the Grays at the other side of the table were aware that something was wrong. 'What ails the boy?' asked Mr Gray. He sounded genuinely concerned.

'He's drunk,' said Will. 'Boy can't handle the hard stuff. Should have stuck to ale.' He was looking daggers at Billy now, as though warning him to handle the situation.

191

Billy threw a powerful arm around Tom's shoulders. 'It's just a wee misunderstanding,' he explained to the others. He used his other hand to prise the copper spoon from Tom's fingers and returned it and the snuffbox to his waistcoat pocket. 'I think I might take the lad outside for a bit of fresh air.'

'Good idea,' said Will.

'No,' hissed Tom. 'I don't need air. I . . .'

Billy leaned in close to whisper in his ear. 'Shut your noise,' he said, 'or by God, I'll break your neck right here and now.' He half-pulled, half-lifted Tom out of his chair.

'Just a moment,' said Mr Gray, getting up out of his own seat.

Billy turned back warily . 'Yes?' he murmured.

Mr Gray raised his tankard of ale. 'Before you go, I'd like to propose a toast. To our genial hosts,' he said, looking first to Billy and then to Will. 'To Mr Burke and Mr Hare.'

Tom felt as though he'd been punched in the stomach. The breath went out of him and he stood there in Billy's clutches, gasping. Suddenly, it all became clear, how naïve, how trusting, how *stupid* he'd been. He didn't know very much about the activities of Burke and Hare, but he was aware of their names. He knew enough to realise that they were murderers and he had blundered into their clutches. And then his head filled with an image, the dream he'd had about Jamie. He saw his friend's terrified face, yelling two words at him as if trying to send a warning. He hadn't been saying 'bird' and 'hay.' Not even close.

Terror flooded Tom now and he made a last attempt to pull free of Billy's clutches, but the powerful man had him in a deadly embrace.

'We'll go then,' he said calmly. 'We'll go over to my place.' He pulled Tom away from the table and through the crowd. Tom found himself surrounded by laughing, jeering faces. Drinks were held aloft as people made toasts to this most evil of nights. The awful music kept up its incessant caterwauling, hands clapped along, feet stamped out a rhythm on the floorboards and not one person seemed to notice that Tom was Billy's prisoner.

'Help me!' he yelled, looking desperately around. 'Please, this man is a . . .'

Billy's forehead came down hard against his own and the world seemed to shudder and shimmer as fireworks exploded in front of him, fireworks mingled with a succession of frantic images – the plague doctor flapping after him along an Edinburgh street, Jamie spooning snuff into his nose and grinning maniacally, Cat smiling at him as she squeezed his hand and then the coffins . . . the tiny wooden coffins, marching away ahead of him in silent single file. It was the last thing he saw before he fell down into darkness . . .

Nineteen

He came slowly, painfully back to consciousness and found he was sitting upright, propped against what felt like a wall. His head hammered with pain and he had to blink several times to bring his vision back into focus. He was in a small, cheerless room, empty aside from a double bed, a wardrobe and a rickety chest of drawers with a framed wooden mirror standing on it. He tried to move and found that he couldn't. It took him a few moments to understand that his hands were tied behind his back and that they had been secured to something he couldn't see.

Any hopes he might have nurtured that he'd somehow moved on to another place and time evaporated in an instant. He was pretty sure that this was Billy and Nell's bedroom in the new lodgings, the place they had taken Mary Docherty to. He looked frantically around. If that was the case, where was she? He noticed something sticking out from beneath the foot of the bed. A pair of stockinged feet. The woman was so drunk, she had somehow managed to wind up *under* the bed instead of in it . . .

'Mary!' he said, urgently. 'Mary Docherty, wake up. You've got to untie me!' There was no reaction so he stretched his legs out as far as he could and jabbed one of her feet with the toe of his shoe. 'Mary, the men that run this place, they're . . .' His voice trailed away as he realised with a dull stab of shock that Mary wasn't going to wake up anytime soon. Her body was too still for someone who might be alive.

Fear jolted through his veins like adrenalin. He started pulling frantically against the ropes that tied him, desperate to escape, but they wouldn't yield an inch. He was trapped, and at any moment Billy Burke and Will Hare might be back to finish him off.

He froze as he heard the sharp metallic click of a key turning in the latch. The door opened and somebody stepped inside. He let out a sigh of relief when he realised it was Nell. He'd never been so glad to see anyone in his entire life.

'Nell!' he gasped. 'You've got to help me, I . . .'

'Shut up!' she hissed, sounding quite unlike herself, her voice as hard and as cold as a fall of January snow. She reached into her dress and pulled out a knife. Her face grim, she came slowly towards him.

'Nell, please, no,' he said. 'You can't . . .'

'Quiet, I said!' Now she was kneeling beside him. She reached around to saw through the rope that bound him. He gave a gasp of relief as his hands came free and looking back, he saw that they'd been tied to a stout metal stanchion set deep into the wall.

'Nell,' he said. 'Billy and Will, they're murderers.'

'I know,' she assured him. 'I've known for the best part of a year.'

'You . . . you knew about it?' He stared at her in disbelief. 'Then why . . .?'

'There's no time to discuss it. You need to get out of here,' she advised him. 'Before they come back.'

'But Nell!' Tom was trying to understand. 'Jamie. They killed Jamie. How could you let them?'

'So, the mother hen's come to look after the chick,' said a familiar voice and Tom looked up in dismay, to see that Billy and Will had entered the room. Billy was carrying a heavy blanket and Tom remembered the time he had woken in the stable to find Billy pushing a blanket into his face. 'Sure, Nell, I had a feeling you might do something stupid.'

'Billy,' said Nell. 'You can't do this. Please!' She got to her feet and approached him. 'He's just a wee boy. He can't do us any harm.'

Billy was smiling as warmly as ever. 'Ah, if only that were so. But he knows too much, Nell. And sure, he won't be the first youngster we've had to deal with.'

Will was closing the door now, turning the key in the lock to ensure they wouldn't be overheard.

Nell was shaking her head. 'I've helped you this far,' she said. 'And God knows, I haven't ridden easy over some of the things we've done. But I won't be a party to this.'

'Then get out,' said Billy, coldly. 'And leave it to us.' He came closer, the blanket held ready.

'You're not touching him,' said Nell. 'I won't allow it.'

'Will you not?' Billy looked genuinely regretful. 'In that case, my love, you leave me no alternative. Let's forget the whole thing.' He made as if to turn away, but at the last moment he swung back round and hit her hard with the flat of his hand, knocking her off her feet and sending her crashing against the metal foot of the bed. She groaned, rolled away and lay still.

'You coward!' snarled Tom, and he scrambled to his feet. 'Hitting a woman.'

Billy shrugged. 'I didn't like doin' it. But some things are necessary, Tom.' He shook his head. 'Ah, why did you have to go asking so many questions?' he lamented with what sounded like genuine regret. 'I really liked you, lad. Which makes what I have to do now all the harder.'

'Get on with it,' snapped Hare. 'Finish the little snitch and let's be done.'

Tom squared desperately up to Billy, his fists raised. 'You come any closer and I'll . . . smash your face in.'

'Oh, planning to make a fight of it are we?' said Billy, amused. 'Let's hope you don't put up the kind of resistance that Jamie did. He was a tough ould nut to crack, so he was. He wouldn't drink enough whisky, see.'

Tom remembered the bruises and cuts he'd seen on Billy's face that day on Tanner's Close. 'You . . . you scumbag!' he snarled. 'You filthy, horrible . . . I'm glad he fought you. I wish he'd punched your teeth out. What did Jamie ever do to you? Huh? Tell me that.'

'He found out things,' said Billy. 'And he started

shooting off that big mouth of his. I warned him about blathering, time and time again, but he paid me no heed.' Billy was holding out the blanket now, looking for an opening. 'Tom, you understand this is nothing personal. It's business.'

'Finish him!' snarled Hare. 'We're missing good drinking time here.'

'Hold your horses,' said Burke. 'I'll do this at my own pace. You go on down if it bothers you. You never were much use at this side of it, were you?'

'I've done my share,' said Will. 'Now for pity's sake, man, get to it.'

'Wait!' said Tom, panicking. 'Listen to me, both of you. You don't have to do this. You really don't. See, I'm from the future. Any minute now, I'll be going back there and . . . I'll never be able to tell anyone what you did.'

'What are you babbling about?' sneered Billy. 'Maybe the boy is drunk.'

'I'm not drunk. I'm just trying to tell you—'

He broke off as Billy made a quick feint to his left. Tom reacted instinctively, but Billy went the other way and ran forward, the blanket raised to cover Tom's face.

And that's when the door of the room exploded inward, smashed by a prodigious force, enough to shatter the lock and send it flying into the room. Billy and Will swung around in shocked surprise as a cloaked, masked figure strode into the room, iron-shod boots clumping on the bare floorboards.

'Who in the name of Lucifer are you?' gasped Billy.

'Step away from the boy,' growled McSweeny, his voice muffled beneath the mask. 'He's mine.'

'I think you'll find he's *ours*,' argued Billy, completely misunderstanding. 'You're not taking him anywhere.' He and Hare squared up to the masked figure and the three of them circled each other warily, looking for an opening. Suddenly, as if commanded, they closed on each other in a flailing, punching frenzy. Tom cowered beside the window, telling himself that whoever won the fight, he was doomed anyway.

In the midst of the frenzy there was movement at the doorway. 'Excuse me, I think I left my stockings . . .'

The voice trailed off in amazement. Tom saw Mrs Gray standing there, open-mouthed in amazement. Her gaze swept around the room, taking in the three wrestling figures and Nell sprawled unconscious on the floor. Her eyes widened as she noticed the stockinged feet jutting out from the foot of the bed. She said something that Tom didn't quite catch and then turned and ran along the corridor beyond, shrieking the word 'Murder!'

The three fighting men were insensible to what had just happened and Tom had no time to wait around to see if Mrs Gray's cries summoned any help. His three adversaries were in the middle of the room, blocking the doorway, and there was only one possible avenue of escape. Tom ran to the room's only window and tried to open it, but the metal catch was rusted shut. He cursed, turned back to the sideboard and snatched up the heavy wooden mirror. He spun around and threw it with all his strength at the window. There was a sudden shattering of glass and a rush of chill air into the room. Tom used his elbow to knock out any remaining chunks of glass around the frame and looked out. Only now did he realise that he was up on the first floor, but he began to climb out anyway. He was halfway through the opening when a hand grabbed at his shoulder and he turned to see Billy, still grinning maniacally, as he attempted to pull Tom back into the room.

'Leaving so soon?' he sneered. Just then a gloved hand closed around Billy's throat, pulling him back, and Tom was free again. He scrambled through the window, looking frantically around for a handhold, knowing that a fall from this height would almost certainly result in broken bones. He caught a glimpse of a cast iron drainpipe to his left and grabbing it with both hands, swung his body around and gripped it with his knees. He began to slide down the pipe and in the same instant a masked face appeared at the broken window above him and a muffled voice bellowed his name. Behind McSweeny a volley of shouts and curses told Tom that Billy and Will were still very much alive.

Galvanised, Tom let go of the drainpipe and dropped the remaining distance to the ground. He landed on his feet and crouched to absorb the impact, but as he straightened up he was horribly aware of McSweeny's huge frame pushing through the window and leaping the full distance to the ground. Tom didn't wait around to see him land. He turned and ran for his life, up the narrow alley and onto Tanner's Close. He turned left and carried on running, looking desperately around for somebody who might help him, but the street was deserted and the sound of heavy, metal-shod boots behind him told him that McSweeny was closing on him fast. To his right he saw a set of wooden double doors and caught sight of a crudely-made sign with 'Tannery' scrawled on it. A length of chain dangled from the latch as though someone had forgotten to lock up for the night. Tom shouldered the door open and ran inside, not knowing what he might find within, only seeking somewhere to hide.

The stench in the place was overpowering, a hideous mingling of urine, dung and acidic chemicals. In the dim moonlight, filtering in through a skylight, he could see scores of what looked like animal hides, hanging on lines of rope, and the wall to his right was decorated with the heads of horned cattle, staring sullenly down at him with blank glass eyes. To his left, a rickety wooden staircase beckoned and he pounded up it, aware as he did so that McSweeny was already pushing his way through the doorway.

'Still running, Tom?' he yelled. 'You can't run forever.'

Tom reached a narrow wooden gantry that extended over a series of huge vats in which unknown chemicals bubbled and seethed. The concentrated stench made it difficult to breathe up there. Chest-high wooden handrails flanked the gantry to prevent accidents. Tom started walking forward in the uncertain light and saw to his horror that ahead of him the walkway was attached to a solid brick wall. He had reached a dead end. He stood there, looking desperately this way and that, all too aware of the sounds of footsteps thudding up the wooden stairs behind him and for a moment he was lost, frozen, shaking in submissive terror. *Maybe*, he thought, *it was best to bow to the inevitable, allow McSweeny to finish him off and put an end to all this endless chasing around through space and time.* All at once he noticed a wooden implement hanging from a hook on one side of the gantry; a stout wooden club, the length of a baseball bat, and fresh hope sprang up in him. He grabbed the club and turned back to face the staircase, the weapon clutched behind his back.

McSweeny crested the stairs and stepped onto the gantry. He reached up a gloved hand and lifted the leather mask from his face to reveal his sweating features. He grinned his mirthless grin as he advanced slowly along the walkway, throwing the mask aside.

'So, Tom,' he croaked. 'Finally, there's nowhere left to run. There's just you and me, as it was always meant to be.'

Tom stayed very still, looking defiantly back at McSweeny. 'I'm glad,' he said, and he was surprised to find that his voice was clear and steady. 'I'm sick of running. We need to finish this.'

McSweeny chuckled. 'I'm glad you feel like that,' he said. 'I'm tired of chasing you too, if you want to know the truth. You've eluded me twice now, but you won't be so lucky this time.'

'We'll see,' said Tom.

McSweeny kept walking and as he did, he reached into the secret place in his cloak. His gloved hand withdrew a steel blade. Tom felt terror stirring within him, like a snake coiling in its lair, but he refused to give in to it. His grip tightened on the handle of the club.

'What have you got behind your back, Tom?' murmured McSweeny. 'Let me have a look.'

Tom flinched, realising he'd lost the element of surprise. Defiantly he brought the club around to where McSweeny could see it.

He laughed derisively. 'What do you think you're going to do with that wee toy?' he mocked.

'Isn't it obvious?' asked Tom, and he grinned right back. 'I'm going to smash your stupid head in.' And with that he started walking forward.

McSweeny's smile faltered. Suddenly, he didn't seem quite so sure of himself. 'You . . . you think you can beat me?' he roared.

'I know I can,' said Tom. 'Because you're a stinking coward who preys on the weak. I'm Tom Afflick and I'm worth twenty of you.'

McSweeny had stopped in his tracks. He brandished the knife. 'You insolent little puppy,' he said. 'I'll cut you to pieces.'

'Come on then,' suggested Tom. 'What are you waiting for?'

McSweeny's eyes blazed with anger. He gave a yell and ran forward, the knife held ready to strike, but Tom stayed stock still, waiting, waiting for the right moment. As the blade swung down at him, he leaned back on his heels and the tip of the knife scythed past, inches from his face. He swung the club out to his right then brought it back in a deadly arc, putting all his strength behind the blow, aiming for the side of McSweeny's head. At the last instant, McSweeny dodged aside and the club missed him completely. It swung downwards, the momentum unbalancing Tom, and thudded against ithe handrail where McSweeny had been standing, splintering the ancient wood with a loud crack.

McSweeny gave a triumphant yell and swung the knife back again. Tom ducked and the blade skimmed above his head, throwing McSweeny off kilter. He grasped at the wooden rail to steady himself. And that was when Tom leapt into the air and drove a foot hard into McSweeny's chest, knocking him backwards against the rail. He rested there a moment, a look of indignation on his face, the breath punched out of him. Then there was a sharp, splintering noise as the shattered wood behind him began to surrender to his weight. McSweeny's eyes widened as he realised what was about to happen. The knife dropped from his grasp and he made a desperate attempt to steady himself, waving his arms like a madman, but he had already lost his fight with gravity.

The handrail parted and McSweeny fell backwards. He dropped ten feet into the bubbling wooden vat below him, hit the soupy liquid with a dull squelch and disappeared under the surface. An instant later he thrashed his way back up again, spluttering and fighting to stay afloat. His entry into the liquid had released a great wave of acidic gas and Tom was obliged to cover his mouth and nose to prevent the gas from filling his lungs. McSweeny stared up at him in absolute hatred. And then he began to scream, clutching at his eyes, tearing at his face, thrashing around in agony. That was when Tom saw a single word chalked onto the side of the tub.

Quicklime.

He had to turn away then because McSweeny's features were melting like hot butter, dissolving into the fluid all around him, and as much as he hated the man, he didn't want to stick around to watch that. He dropped the club and hurried back along the gantry. McSweeny was still screaming as Tom pounded down the steps, but he'd stopped by the time Tom made it outside. Once there he drew gulps of fresh air into his lungs and began to walk away. He was horribly aware of a tide of nausea rising within him and after a few steps he began to retch. He leaned up against a wall and vomited the badness out of him and only when he had rid himself of every last bit of sickness did he walk on, moving in the opposite direction to Laird's and heading for the only place where he thought he'd be safe. The McCallum's.

Twenty

Even Mr McCallum couldn't complain about taking in a boy in such a dire predicament. Tom was allowed to sleep on a temporary bed that Mary made up for him in the kitchen. Over the next few days Tanners Close erupted with the news of the grisly happenings at Laird's Lodging House, which soon became widely known as the West Port Murders. Fraser kept going out and coming back with the latest information.

Mrs Gray had done her duty and reported the strange goings-on she'd witnessed in Burke's lodgings to the constables, although she claimed that shortly afterwards, Nell had sought her out and offered her a bribe of £10 a week to keep quiet about the matter. Mrs Gray told the constables that she'd seen Burke and Hare fighting in Burke's room, but oddly, she made no mention of the cloaked and masked figure they were struggling with. She had, however, noticed the little matter of a dead body lying under the bed. Shortly afterwards, an anonymous tip-off had led the constables to Surgeons' Hall where Mary Docherty's corpse had been found lying on a trolley, only moments before Doctor Knox and his assistants were due to start dissecting it.

Burke and Hare were promptly arrested, along with their common-law wives, Nell McDougal and

Margaret Laird. Now the four of them languished in jail awaiting trial. The tally of victims quickly began to mount. Mrs Docherty, of course, was the first name to be confirmed, shortly followed by poor Jamie. Then Mary and Peggy Haldane. As the days unfolded, more and more mysterious disappearances were finally explained.

It was Cat who came up with the idea.

'All those poor helpless people,' she told Tom, 'Not one of them given a decent Christian burial. We can't let that go unmarked. We have to do something.' So Fraser's little coffins were called into service and as the tally mounted, so he was obliged to make more and more of them, working late into the night to ensure there would be enough for all of the victims. However, even though Cat pointed out that many of the victims had been female, Fraser still stubbornly refused to allow her to dress any of them accordingly.

'They're still soldiers to me,' he insisted, 'and if you want me to help you, you'll have to accept that.'

In the end Cat had reluctantly agreed. She took extra care with one particular soldier though, dressing him in a white linen suit. 'This one is Jamie,' she told Tom, 'and I've made him look like an angel, because I'm sure that's what he must be by now.'

Tom had nodded, but he knew only too well, that whatever Jamie Wilson had done in life, it certainly wouldn't qualify him for angelhood.

Fraser certainly had his work cut out. When the murdering duo's first victim came to light, he turned out to have been an old lodger called Donald who had died of natural causes nearly a year before, owing Will rent. It had been then that Billy and Will had first hit on the idea of selling the body to the surgeons for dissection. They'd received the sum of £7.10s for their trouble. After making such easy money, they hadn't felt inclined to wait for nature to take its course again and instead had started picking off easy targets – preying on the homeless, the unloved, those who simply wouldn't be missed. In the end, of course, it had been Jamie who had proved to be a step too far for Burke and Hare. He was too well-known to be swept under the carpet. Mary Docherty's corpse was simply confirmation of their crimes, but questions had already begun to be asked when a student at Surgeons' Hall had recognised Jamie's corpse.

Doctor Knox was too distinguished and too wealthy to ever be convicted of anything, but the general feeling was that he must have known there was something suspicious about the steady supply of fresh bodies Burke and Hare had supplied him with. He had either ignored his suspicions or simply hadn't cared. People muttered darkly about him in pubs and shop doorways and referred to him as 'Knox the butcher.'

Eventually, after Burke had made a full confession, Fraser had his final count. Seventeen innocent victims dissected under the cold, sharp knives of the Edinburgh surgeons. There was some discussion about whether old Donald should be afforded a coffin of his own as he wasn't technically a murder victim, but Cat had insisted.

'He was dissected like the rest of them,' she said. 'And he had nobody to stand at his grave and mourn him. We can't leave him out.' So he too was added to the list. In the end, Tom was needed to help with the work and made three coffins himself, though he would have been the first to admit that he didn't make quite so neat a job of it as Fraser. As he worked, he couldn't help but think how amazing this was. He was working on a set of coffins that would be on display in the National Museum of Scotland in the 21st century. When he had first set eyes upon them he had no idea that he had actually *made* some of them. Part of him longed to tell Cat and Fraser about it, but he realised that there was only so much they could accept. So he worked on in silence.

Finally, one day in January, everything was ready. Tom, Cat and Fraser set off for Arthur's Seat, wrapped up tight against the cold and carrying the tiny coffins, carefully wrapped in a knapsack. They took with them a couple of trowels and a sharp knife. They spent some time searching for the best spot and finally found a small opening on the north-eastern slopes, a natural recess which Fraser and Tom hollowed out a little more with their trowels, clearing out the soil and lining the sides with pieces of slate. It soon became clear that the opening wasn't wide enough to lay out all the coffins in a single row so Fraser found more pieces of slate and cut them roughly to size to construct two tiers of eight coffins each, with Jamie's coffin given pride of place on its own at the very top. Once they had everything in place they blocked up the opening with carefully selected stones and placed sods of earth over them. Then Cat said a prayer, speaking the words clearly and respectfully, her eyes brimming with tears.

When they had finished Fraser announced that he needed to get back to hear the latest news on Burke and Hare and he left Cat and Tom standing by the coffins' hiding place.

'It's good to think that they'll be here for ever, looking down on the city,' said Cat.

Tom didn't have the heart to tell her that they would be discovered in just eight years time and that more than half of Fraser's carefully constructed coffins would be destroyed by a gang of stupid boys who would spend their time throwing them at each other. He supposed that when the coffins were found, she might hear about it herself and he wondered why she and Fraser had never come forward to claim ownership of them. Perhaps they'd simply decided that a good mystery was worth preserving. He would have have liked to tell Cat that some of the coffins, Jamie's amongst them, would end up in the National Museum of Scotland where future generations of people would come to view them; that students of history would speculate about their meaning and about who put them into the little hiding place on Arthur's Seat.

They stood on the hillside and looked out over the city, Tom thinking about how what was little more than a village would grow steadily over the years into the great, grey stone capital that he would visit in the twenty first century. He'd been feeling strange all morning, a woozy, rushing sensation in his head, and he wondered if something weird was going to happen. He was beginning to feel as though his time here was rapidly running out.

'It's great up here,' he said. 'You can see pretty much the entire city.'

But Cat seemed to want to talk about something else. She took his hands in hers and held them tightly as she looked at him, the tears still in her eyes.

'Tom,' she murmured. 'With everything that's been going on, we've lost sight of something.'

He looked at her puzzled. 'What's that?'

'If what you told me is true . . . and I believe it is, about you coming from the future and everything, then you're going to be leaving us one of these days. And I don't know if I can stand to lose you.'

He smiled at her. 'I don't really have any control over that,' he said. 'To tell you the truth, I'm feeling kind of like it might happen sometime soon.'

Her eyes widened. 'I hope that's not true,' she said.

'Right now, if I had a choice, I wouldn't want to leave.'

'Why's that?' she asked him.

'Because I've found something worth staying for,' he said.

And he took her in his arms and held her tightly.

It was only a short time later, as they began to descend the slope, that the drifting, swirling feeling within him began to grow stronger. He was looking out at the world, but it was beginning to look transparent, as though he was barely there. He called Cat's name. She was walking the narrow trail ahead of him and she looked back in alarm.

'Tom?' she cried. 'What's wrong?'

'I don't know . . . I . . . I think . . . it's happening'

She rushed back to hold him in her arms. 'Not yet,' she pleaded. 'Please, don't go. Stay a little longer.'

But she was already fading from his sight. He tried to pull her to him and she crumpled beneath his hands like confetti, blown in the wind. Then he was falling and this time he knew he was going back and there was nothing he could do to stop himself.

Twenty-one

'Tom! Tom, are you all right? Say something!'

Slowly, painfully, he opened his eyes. At first he saw nothing but a meaningless blur of colour swimming in front of him. Then his mother's face came into focus. She was leaning over him and she looked scared.

He realised that he was back in the museum. He was sitting propped against a wall and his head hurt really badly. He glanced down at himself and saw that he was dressed in his own clothes although they were grubby and torn, but Mum didn't seem to have noticed that for the moment. A figure moved into view behind Mum. Hamish. But it was 21st century Hamish, dressed in his anorak and jeans and he looked contrite.

'I didn't mean to hurt him,' he said. 'I was just . . .'

Mum turned on him. 'You get away from him,' she snarled. 'Haven't you done enough damage for one day?'

'I only meant to push him,' insisted Hamish.

'You're drunk,' said Mum. She turned back to Tom. 'Shall I go and get help?' she asked him.

'No,' he said. 'I'm all right.' Leaning his weight against the wall, he managed to pull himself upright. He lifted a hand to the back of his head and his fingers came away red with blood.

'I really didn't mean to do that,' insisted Hamish.

'I've had a few drinks, but I'm not drunk. Not really.' He was wringing his hands, clearly dismayed by what had happened. 'Please,' he said. 'Catherine.' He stepped forward and put a hand on Mum's shoulder, but she shrugged it away.

Tom gathered his senses around him. He took a step forward and pushed Hamish in the chest, making him take a step back. 'Listen to me,' he said. 'It's time we had a talk. I know who you are. I know what goes on in your head.'

Hamish's mouth dropped open. 'What are you . . .?'

'I said *listen*. You're going to shape up. You're going to stop messing Mum around. If you don't, she'll leave you and then where will you be?'

Hamish looked flustered. He tried to protest. 'You can't just . . .'

'Yes, I can,' interrupted Tom. His head was still throbbing but he was determined to say his piece. 'Mum deserves better than this. So you're going to stop the boozing and you're going to treat her properly or you'll have me to answer to. Understand?'

Hamish gasped like a fish out of water. 'I . . . you're just a kid, you can't . . .'

Tom lifted a hand to silence him. 'You're done,' he said. 'Now get off to your stupid football match and leave us in peace.'

There was a long silence. Hamish stood there, gazing back at Tom and it seemed as though his face flickered momentarily. Just for a second, a leaner, meaner face glared back at Tom, but then it was gone, replaced by its more hapless modern equivalent. Hamish nodded. He seemed to accept what had been said. He looked at Mum. 'I'm sorry,' he said and it sounded genuine. He turned and walked away and kept going until he reached the swing doors at the top of the room. He pushed through them and was gone.

Mum stared at Tom, as though he'd just pulled off the most amazing magic trick in history. 'He . . . he did what you said,' she gasped. 'And he's been drinking.'

Tom shrugged. 'He needs to get his act together,' he said. He felt totally in control if the situation.

'You know, don't you, that he's not always like that?' argued Mum. 'It's only when he's had a few drinks. The rest of the time, he's a pussy cat. Honestly.'

'I don't care,' said Tom. 'You can't let him mess you around any more. You need to tell him what you want and he has to agree. Otherwise, tell him to go to hell and find somebody else. And then, maybe you can move on with your life.' He fixed her with a look. 'Dad's moved on and you've got to do the same.'

They stood there looking at each other in silence for a moment. Then Mum said. 'Are you sure you're ok?'

He nodded. 'I'm good,' he assured her. And he meant it. He had never felt more positive, more in control of his life. He looked at the display cabinet that held the tiny coffins and noticed a smear of blood on one corner of it. He reached up his sleeve to wipe it clean. He was glad to see that the three coffins he'd made had, against all the odds, survived. He could pick them out instantly by the rounded corners. Better still, Jamie was still there, dressed in his all-white suit of clothes. Tom smiled. 'Angel Jamie,' he muttered, remembering something that Cat had said. Mum's shrill voice alerted him to the fact that she'd finally noticed that something was amiss.

'Tom . . . your clothes!'

'Hmm? What about them?'

'I didn't notice before that they were so . . . dirty.' She leaned forward and sniffed at him, then made a face. 'They need to go in the washer.' She studied him. 'Actually, that jacket looks like it should go to the charity shop.'

Tom looked down again. Proof, he decided. Proof that he really had been sleeping rough in a filthy stable at Laird's Lodging House. He thought of something else. He reached into his pocket and pulled out his mobile phone. The battery power was exactly as it had been when he'd arrived at the museum. Weird. He hit the camera icon and looked at his most recent pictures. There they were, three new shots of Edinburgh. Mum was looking at them over her shoulder. 'When did you take those?' she asked him.

'Oh, just the other day,' he told her. The first shot was the best. It showed Jamie, looking quizzically at the camera, his mouth open as though he was asking a question.

'Who's that?' asked Mum.

Tom smiled. 'Just somebody I met,' he told her. The other two shots, one of the street and one of the castle, he realised, could pretty much have been taken at any time in history. There was nothing there to date them. He quickly emailed the first photograph to himself, hoping against hope that when he opened the image back on his computer in Manchester it wouldn't just be a plain grey rectangle like it had been last time.

Mum sighed. 'Well,' she said, 'if you're absolutely sure you don't need to see a doctor or anything . . .'

'I'm good, really,' he assured her, but when he thought of his final moments back in the 19th century, it was with a sense of sadness. He could see Cat, reaching for him, calling his name.

'You were telling me before Hamish turned up that you were hungry,' said Mum. 'You want to go and eat something?'

'Sure.' He ran his hand across the top of the glass cabinet one last time and whispered, 'Bye, Jamie.' And he thought he would get a big slab of chocolate cake with his coffee and he'd think about Jamie while he ate it.

He was about to start walking away when something caught his attention. A large oil painting hanging on the far wall, something that he was fairly sure hadn't been there before. 'Just a minute,' he said. He crossed the room, threading his way between the glass cabinets until he was standing directly in front of the painting. It was a portrait of a middle-aged woman, dressed in

19th century clothing, her blonde hair arranged in an elaborate coiffure. She was good-looking rather than pretty, with strong features and a confident smile. The green eyes were exactly as he remembered them. She gazed out of the picture across the centuries and Tom felt that she could somehow see him, back here, where he really belonged. Even though she must have been twenty or thirty years older than when he'd last seen her, he'd recognised her instantly. The picture had a small plaque beneath it.

Catriona McCallum 1813-1882

Beneath the portrait, there was a glass case and arranged within it were a series of very familiar-looking notebooks. Tom smiled as he read the information card that lay in the case beside the books.

Catriona McCallum's early diaries, begun when she was just thirteen years old, have given historians a unique insight into 19th century Edinburgh. Raised in West Port (a stone's throw from the lodging house where Burke and Hare enacted their ghastly crimes), Catriona's accounts of everyday city life offer a fascinating view of the Edinburgh of its day and her use of language is sometimes particularly experimental for its time. She went on to publish several novels, including The Path of Truth (1836) and Walking In Eden (1842). A great deal of interest has centred on

what appears to be an unpublished novel entitled The
Traveller In Time which predates the work of 'father of
science-fiction', Jules Verne, by decades. The book tells
of a young boy from a futuristic Manchester who finds
himself transported to the Edinburgh of 1824. Whether
she ever sought publication for the story is unclear, but
scholars have been intrigued by the book's dedication,
which reads, simply: To Tom. Forever.

Tom smiled and looked back up at the picture.

'You made it, Cat,' he said. 'Just like I said you would.'

Mum looked at him, clearly worried. 'I'm really not sure you're ok,' she said. 'You seem to be rambling. Don't you think we should get you over to the hospital and have you checked out?'

He turned and smiled at her. 'You worry too much,' he told her. 'I've never felt better. Come on, let's go and eat.'

Mum turned and he followed her towards the exit. From the picture, Cat's gaze watched him every step of the way.

Afterword

William 'Billy' Burke was tried initially on just one murder, that of Mary Docherty. His early testimony tells of a mysterious stranger who entered the room and left the old woman's body under the bed. Nobody took it seriously. Throughout the trial he insisted that Nell McDougal was not involved in the murders. Burke was convicted and sentenced to death. He was hanged at 8.15 am on the 28th January 1828, at the Lawnmarket, Edinburgh, in front of a crowd of 20-25,000 people. Seats in tenements that had a view of the scaffold exchanged hands for between five shillings to one pound, displaying a spirit of enterprise that Burke would no doubt have approved of.

The following day his body was dissected at University Old College. Tickets were available for that 'event' too and there was a near-riot when it was found that the seats had been oversold. The dissection lasted two hours, during which Professor Munro dipped a quill pen into Burke's blood and wrote on a pice of paper; *This is written with the blood of Wm Burke, who was hanged at Edinburgh. This blood was taken from his head.*

Burke's skeleton is still displayed at the University of Edinburgh's Anatomy Museum while his death mask and items made from his tanned skin can be seen at his old place of business, Surgeons' Hall. Wallets supposedly made from his skin were on sale in Edinburgh in the weeks after his execution.

William Hare was offered the opportunity to 'turn Queen's evidence' against Burke, granting him immunity from prosecution. He eagerly took it and gave a full confession, listing all the murders that he and Burke had been party to. This meant that after the trial he was able to walk away with no charges against him, a decision that was (understandably) incredibly unpopular at the time. He was released in February 1829 and headed for Dumfries, but was soon recognised and on his arrival there, found himself surrounded by an angry mob of 8,000 people, all baying for his blood. A police escort took him to out of town, set him down on the Annan Road and instructed him to head for England. He was briefly spotted two miles south of Carlisle and then was never seen again. A popular rumor of the time suggests that a mob of people threw him into a lime pit and that he ended his days as a blind beggar, wandering the streets of London.

Nell McDougall was accorded the uniquely Scottish verdict of 'not proven'. After the trial she returned to her home, but any hopes of returning to her former life were quickly dashed when she found herself besieged by crowds of people. Disguised in men's clothes, she managed to escape to the local police station where she was given protection and from there, decided to try her luck in her hometown of Stirling. But once again she was recognised and pursued. She tried Newcastle with the same results, and then Durham, after which, not much is known about her. A popular rumor claims that she died (possibly in a house fire) in Australia in 1868.

Margaret Laird parted company with William Hare on the Annan Road and after that, much like Nell McDougall, she spent her days moving from place to place, pursued by baying crowds. She first tried Greenock and when that failed, she and her baby were put aboard a boat bound for Belfast. Her intention was to head back to her hometown of Derry, but whether she got there or not, we'll probably never know.

Dr Robert Knox was cleared of all complicity in the murders although this didn't appease the population of Edinburgh. A few days after Burke's execution, the doctor's home was besieged by an armed mob and stones were thrown at his windows. Then an effigy of Knox was hung from a tree on Calton Hill and a bonfire lit beneath it. Knox was forced to flee his home, disguised in his military uniform and armed with pistol and sword. After the heat had died down he continued to lecture on anatomy, but the stigma of Burke and Hare stayed with him and he eventually left Edinburgh and moved to London, where he worked as a medical practitioner in Hackney and later as an anatomist at the Royal Marsden Cancer Hospital in Brompton, until his death in 1862.

The misdeeds of this unholy alliance are probably best remembered in a popular 19th century children's rhyme.

Up the close and down the stair,
In the house with Burke and Hare.
Burke's the butcher, Hare's the thief,
Knox, the boy who buys the beef.